Lady of the Lost Fae

THE STARLING SERIES

DANA LEEANN

Content & Copyright

Ebook ISBN: 979-8-9875602-3-5
Paperback ISBN: 979-8-9875602-4-2
Hardcover ISBN: 979-8-9875602-5-9

Cover by Giulia Wille
Edited by Rocky Calvo (Rocky Edits)
Published by One More Chapter Publishing LLC

For those who dream...

Of a fae high lord lacing his fingers through your hair while he bends you over his massive oak desk.

Chapter One

DREYDEN

Four months and three days have passed since the Tartarus monarchy crumbled to Adeena's uncontrolled wrath, and in that quick blink of time, I've watched Adeena exhaust herself with endless hours of endurance and strength conditioning on top of full-time training with Geras. Her newly found powers have strengthened beyond recognition, beyond what I ever imagined possible, and are becoming increasingly difficult to control. Even though she spends nearly every day aiming to contain the growing energy, I see her slowly slipping into a downward spiral.

The loss of her friends and family has finally caught up to her now that the weight of the prophecy has been lifted from her shoulders, freeing up her mind and allowing her to fall victim to the darkest corners of her imagination. Far too often, I find her sobbing in our bathing chambers when she believes herself to be alone, with no one to hear the sorrowful release of pain she keeps hidden inside. Nightmares wake her nightly, pulling her into a frenzied panic as she finds her way back to the harsh reality she now faces. Silent tears stream down her sweet face as she buries herself into my chest, soaking my skin in the aftermath of each nightmare. She refuses to acknowledge the nightmares when the sun rises following dark nights, but I know denial will only work for so long before it catches up with her. A tidal wave of emotion is coming, and it's only a matter of time until it crashes.

I want to be enough for her, and I want to be the one to save her from herself. I *need* to be the one to save her from herself after everything she lost, but I'm not enough. Her heartache is too great, and can only be cured through her grieving process, which is going to take time... a lot of time, but I can be patient. Four hundred years of life have instilled patience within me, and for my mate, I can wait forever.

As I wait for Adeena to find herself again, I fill my days portaling to and from Tartarus with as many supplies as my magic will carry. Dark times have fallen over Tartarus, darker than I ever thought possible, and I'm doing everything I can to help those who have fallen victim to the corrupt kingdom. Six days a week, I travel with ingredients to bake fresh bread and overstuffed baskets of fiber to weave new fabrics, hoping to replace some of what has been lost, but I can't keep up. My magic is depleted to near empty by the sixth day of each week, forcing me to remain in Fire Court on the seventh day, replenishing my tank and formulating a plan for the week to come. Between attending as many of Adeena's training sessions as I can and trips between Fire Court and Tartarus, I am wearing thin.

Feral wildfires broke out shortly after the war ended, burning down entire villages and leaving most without food, shelter, or even clean drinking water most days. The people of Tartarus are penniless, stuck fending for themselves in a fallen kingdom where they have nothing, and no one is stepping up to end the famine. The blame can't necessarily be placed on anyone considering the animalistic state Tartarus has taken. Obtaining peace and order will take a force greater than I've ever witnessed.

Fleeing isn't a sane option. Tartarus is surrounded by endless seas on all sides but one which, as luck would have it, is the Wychwood Forest. Few dare venture into the somber woods, and we haven't caught word of anyone emerging from the other side into Archai.

Creatures once banished to the forest now seep out, creeping their way into Tartarus as they realize an abandoned border equates to freedom. Wind Court and Land Court continue to hold their ground on the eastern side of the forest, but nothing is being done on the western perimeter.

Tartarus is falling apart, deteriorating daily as its people find themselves increasingly victim to a decaying kingdom, lost and broken without a leader. Erebus may have been one of the most crooked kings Tartarus had ever seen, but at least the kingdom had a sense of order under his rule. The consequences of his death expand far beyond what anyone could have predicted.

My gold-winged spies report back to me in the evenings with news of the chaos and unrest that spreads across the land just as a virus would. Most people are tucked away in hiding, too terrified to emerge out of fear of being caught, stranded in the open, should a band of looters pass through the area.

Crimes go unpunished, bringing out the worst in everyone. A sick purge is sweeping across the land, spinning out of control as criminals take over.

The four courts of Archai once met weekly to discuss regaining control of the land, but the meetings quickly faded to nothing as the other courts realized the monstrosity of the task ahead. No one was up to the job, and frankly, only I cared enough to put the time and resources into it. What surprised me most was Lady Hali's unwillingness to lend resources to the cause. We grew up together, trained together, fought wars together. I thought I knew her character well enough to believe she would assist me in aiding the people of Tartarus, but I was wrong. She turned her head as quickly as Lord Soren and Lord Weylin did, sending me back home to Fire Court filled with disgust and rage. We haven't spoken since, and I don't intend on reaching out any time soon.

My priorities are larger than the desire to mend my friendship with Lady Hali. In addition to my mate's unstable emotional state, I still have my duty as high lord to see that my court runs smoothly, without chaos or trouble, and that the people remain happy.

Izan has stepped up to ensure their basic needs are tended to and that our self-sustainable way of life continues while I'm away, but he cannot handle the entire court by himself.

However, today is a day to put all that aside and focus on my mate.

Adeena's stars shimmer, casting an aura around her naked body as rays of sunshine dance across her soft skin. Her hair is wet, slicked back by the sparkling waters of Caelum Lake, and silver wings gently flutter behind her back, drying in the warm sunlight as she sits atop a flat rock overlooking the jeweled waters. She hums a soft, sweet tune while keeping her eyes closed, lazily resting her head on my lap.

She's the most beautiful creature I've ever seen, and she's mine. How I got so lucky, I'll never know. I thank the gods every day for gifting her to me and for sending her back to me when I thought she had slipped through my fingers, gone forever, and lost to uncontrolled rage.

My world stopped spinning and my heart ceased to beat when I held her lifeless body in my arms. Sometimes I still find myself broken, lost in an empty space as I replay the memory.

I shake my head, pushing away my thoughts before they become too dark, ruining my good mood and what is supposed to be a quiet day off with Adeena. A day to reconnect, to slow down for a moment.

Adeena's muscles flex in her forearm as she pushes off her stomach, sitting up before turning to look at me through sterling silver eyes. "I'm hungry," she groans as she summons her wings back into her body, slipping a loose tunic over her head as they fold.

I laugh, softly grinning as I tease my mate, "You're always hungry."

Over-exertion is the source of her extreme hunger, but I didn't dare confront her about it when she was already so unstable. That conversation was for another day, and I know neither of us are ready for it right now.

Twisting to reach the basket hidden behind me, I watch Adeena's face light up as I pull the surprise into view.

"You brought lunch?" she squeals with excitement.

"Do you think I don't know you well enough to assume you'd be starving after a long hike and a full morning of swimming?" I raise my brow, challenging her judgment.

She eyes me up and down, and I can tell she's trying to come up with a witty response, but the sight of food clouds her mind. She sighs before flashing me a mischievous smile. "What'd you bring me?"

Reaching into the basket, I pull out a cluster of plump green grapes and a loaf of sticky, honey-brushed bread. Sugary sweets are one of the many ways I edge my way deeper into Adeena's tender heart.

Adeena clasps her hands together, scooting closer before she swipes the bread from my grasp. "Did Thea make these? I thought I smelled something sweet baking this morning before we left, and I was worried it would be gone by the time we arrived back." Her eyes flutter closed as her teeth sink into the tip of the loaf, hungrily tearing at the flaky crust. "Mmm," she moans as the honey-brushed bread coats her tongue.

My heart rate picks up at the sight of her happiness. It's such a small gesture, yet a wide smile spreads across her soft lips, warming me as I behold the first genuinely real smile I've seen from her in weeks. It's a sight I tirelessly crave, and I've been starved of it too much lately.

"Your smile is beautiful," I whisper next to her ear as I press a gentle kiss onto her cheek.

Tucking a stray lock of hair behind her ear, she gives me a shy half-grin. Words don't escape her lips, but her eyes tell me she's appreciative of my compliment. Adeena still hasn't adjusted to the endless shower of compliments and praise I wash over her daily. From what I understand, she was well-loved growing up, and tributes were a large part of her family life. Sometimes my well-intended praise makes her feel warm and cherished, but other times it reminds her of the family she lost. I'm still not sure how to work around it.

I sit quietly while watching Adeena devour the bread and fruit. Her small hands pluck the green grapes one at a time, popping them into her open mouth as soon as it's ready for the next one.

"Are you ready to head back? I thought we could spend the afternoon enjoying each other's company from the comfort of our bed." My words are low, softly caressing the tender part of her neck as they pass over her. I can see her shoulders roll back ever so slightly, dropping into a more relaxed position.

She turns her cheek into mine, leaning closer as she says, "As much as I would love that, *high lord,* I have other plans for us."

I rub my hand over my trousers as her words harden my cock. She knows what those two words do to me, and she constantly uses them to get what she wants, and I am not ashamed to admit it works every time.

Her sterling eyes drift lower, landing on my hand as it presses into my cock. Those gorgeous eyes fill with desire as she licks her bottom lip, trying her best to maintain focus. She struggles to drag her eyes back to my face.

"Oh?" I smile, stroking her jaw with my thumb. "And what are those other plans? What could be more important than *this*?" I ask as I point to the growing bulge in my trousers.

"I've been working on something while you've been away in Tartarus." She jumps to her feet, quickly pulling on her trousers and boots. "Stand up, I want to show you."

I rise, standing next to her, unsure of what she's about to show me. "Here?"

"Yes, here," she rolls her eyes at my curious question. "Back up."

A sly smile washes across my lips. "I like it when you tell me what to do," I growl as I take three steps back. Her gentle eyes watch me, patiently waiting for me to obey. "Is this far enough?"

She nods, taking a step away from me. "Yes. It's not perfect, but I finally feel like I'm good enough to show you."

My heart sinks a little. The thought of my mate feeling like she must be proficient at anything before she shows me doesn't sit well with me. I want to see and hear about everything she does, and it doesn't matter if she's masterful of the skill or absolute trash. I want to be there for it all. I *need* to be there for it all.

Forcing a smile back to my face as I meet her eyes, I say, "Well I'd love to see whatever it is."

Adeena breathes in deeply, then releases the breath as she steadies her feet. I am unsure of what she's about to do, but I love watching this woman put her all into everything she does.

She takes another step away, inching closer and closer to the edge of the tall rock overlooking the lake.

"You're going to fall," I impulsively remind her.

My fingers stretch at my sides, forming fists, then opening as I try to maintain control of myself.

"Am I?" She raises a brow at me as she continues her path backward.

"If you get any closer to the edge of that rock, you're going to." I take a step closer, naturally feeling the need to save her from falling.

"Mmm, no," she wags her finger at me. "Stay there."

I freeze in place, pushing against every instinct inside me begging to grab her wrist before she falls. I need to be more patient with her. I need to trust she knows what she's doing, even when I have no idea what she's about to do. I silently scold myself for not allowing her the space she needs to be free.

Stopping as close to the edge as she can without falling, she watches me, and I swear I see a hint of adrenaline flush through her irises. Her eyes close for a moment, and I feel a warm wind slip past me as she summons her magic.

Adeena's grand silver wings expand behind her, unfolding as she releases them from her body. They effortlessly slip through slits in her tunic, specially designed for wings like ours. Shimmery silver dust falls around her, reflecting light as it drifts through rays of sunshine.

My breath quickens as I watch the divine beauty that comes with being fae unravel before me. Adeena was lovely as a human, but as a fae, she is other-worldly, a true goddess in the flesh.

Her wings are fully stretched now, fluttering in the breeze created by her magic as it flows through her. I can't help but smile while I watch her.

"Are you ready?" she asks with a grin plastered across her face.

Before I can respond, she's falling backward, plummeting toward the glittering waters below. I rush forward, afraid to see her hit the water with her wings stretched so wide. A fall from this height is guaranteed to break a wing.

"No!" I shout. "Tuck your wings!"

I summon my gold wings, ripping my black tunic in half as they explode from my back.

My heart is in my stomach as I lunge over the edge of the rock.

Chapter Two

ADEENA

I hear him yell for me as I dip out of view, free-falling toward the jeweled waters below. I watch above me, patiently waiting for him.

He does exactly what I predicted he would do. Dreyden's head comes into view as he dives over the rock without a second thought. There's fear in his eyes, and I can tell he regrets obeying my warning to stay back.

What a good mate.

A light-hearted chuckle passes through my lips as his eyes lock with his and he realizes what's happening. His wings flex, spreading behind him like a parachute to stop his descent.

I'm flying, fluttering in place a few feet above the surface of the water. Not only that, but I'm also doing it with *ease.* Flying has been my greatest physical challenge since becoming fae, and I've finally got a small grasp on it. Months of secret flying lessons with Geras have finally paid off.

Geras doesn't even have wings, which made our training sessions even more difficult, but he *does* have several hundred years of expertise in training, combat, and mentorship.

I won't lie, it's been incredibly testing. There have been way too many bruises and bumps along the way, and I've hidden the true reason behind when Dreyden asks by telling him they were from our regular training.

He is skeptical of my training, always threatening Geras behind my back, but Geras and I are closer than he knows. Each time Dreyden corners Geras, obnoxiously reminding him to pull back on the intensity of our training, Geras finds me almost immediately to warn me of Dreyden's piss-poor mood and lack of ability to give me the space I need to find myself again. Dreyden brought Geras to Fire Court in the first place. The least he could do is let me use him as we originally planned.

Even though Dreyden comes on strong, I can't help but love him so deeply it hurts. He's possessive and an asshole, but he's *my* possessive asshole. My mate. His heart is in the right place, but he doesn't know how to trust me and trust that I know best for myself. I have my best interests at heart, and I know how to work through my extreme grief. It's not going to be easy, but I know I can do it. It's just going to take time.

Some people work better under stress and under pressure, and I'm one of them. Pushing my body to its limits physically exhausts me, allowing me to sleep better at night, and think through my problems. Wearing myself thin allows me to prioritize what I'm feeling. To Dreyden it may look like denial, and I know it does because of the familiar look I see in his eyes after a breakdown, but it's not. It's me prioritizing my emotions one at a time, working through them until I feel less and less. There's nothing wrong with allowing myself to feel each emotion wholly and completely. I do it my way, and not many people understand it.

Geras gets it, and that's why he doesn't pull back on the intensity of our training when Dreyden throws a fit. He understands me on a deeper level, and I've begun looking at him as somewhat of a father figure in my life. No one will ever replace the biological father I cherished and loved, but Geras has been there and allowed me to do what I need to when no one else comprehends. Perhaps he looks at me like the daughter he never had, or maybe he sees a little bit of himself in me. Either way, I'm forever grateful for the amount of time he spends helping me perfect my magic, and for the never-ending patience he shows me day after day.

"You can fly?" Dreyden gasps in disbelief as his wings catch his fall. "Who taught you to fly?"

I watch his wide eyes, smiling as I respond, "Geras did. We've been working on it while you've been away in Tartarus. How do I look?"

I shift my body back and forth, pointing to the massive feather wings behind my back. Gold magic dust from Dreyden's wings drifts over me as it falls from above, mixing with silver dust of my own.

The grin on Dreyden's face is enough to make me die happy, and I swear I'll never get enough of it. A giddy, butterfly feeling rolls through my heart, heating my cheeks as it makes me blush.

"You take my breath away, Adeena. It's not often I'm caught speechless, but right now I'm struggling to find words to describe the view before me." He flies lower, slowly approaching me as he is careful not to knock me off balance. "Can we go flying?"

Our eyes meet as he takes my hand in his, gently pulling me into his hard, now shirtless body. His intoxicating scent hits my nose, flowing through me as though it's my blood.

"I thought you'd never ask," I whisper against his cheek as I inhale the woodsy amber fragrance that was my mate.

Dreyden drifts back, stretching our arms to full length before allowing our grasps to carefully slip apart. "Lead the way, *high lady*," he beams at me as he gestures toward the radiant sky above the Bloodred Forest.

Ever since the gods titled me High Lady of the Sky, he has resorted to calling me "high lady" every chance he gets. I haven't told him, and I'm not sure I will, but his words have the same effect on me as when I call him "high lord." The power behind those two short words gets a rise out of me, pulling at something deep within my core. The feeling is primal as it rolls off the tip of his tongue.

I give him an excited smile, his only indicator that I'm about to take off, shooting into the sky with almost as much grace as he has when he flies.

I tuck my chin, watching as he follows closely behind. He keeps up with ease as he watches the view ahead of him.

My ass. Or *his* ass as he likes to call it.

A sea of crimson foliage spreads below us, expanding far beyond the distant horizon. It's high noon and the sun is blazing today, but the breeze between my wings feels magnificent as it slips over my feathers, cooling my body temperature.

Dreyden and I look like shooting stars as we blast through the sky, silver and gold orbs leaving a shimmery dust in our wake. The two of us create a small galaxy of stars, and someday I hope to illuminate our world further with our children. It's a distant dream, but one I will hold onto until I'm ready to make it a reality. Until *we* are ready to make it a reality.

Dreyden and I fly under and over each other, laughing and giggling like children as we soar through the sky.

"How did Geras teach you to fly if he can't fly himself?" Dreyden's voice is full of curiosity as he questions my new skill.

The gold stars stamped across his skin reflect in the light, nearly blinding me, and I quickly adjust my angle before it turns into an accident. That's the last thing I need right now. My bruises from the last failed flight just finished healing. My fae skin has no imperfections for the first time in as long as I can remember, likely as far back as the moment I became fae.

"Geras is patient with me, and he's smart. He has studied the art of fae flight, and I'd be willing to say he knows more about it than you do," I wink at him as I say that last part.

A jealous, low growl rumbles in Dreyden's chest, almost too quiet for my ears to pick up, but I manage to catch it. A mischievous smirk slides across my lips.

Target hit.

He's too easy.

"I could have taught you," he snaps under his breath.

I change my pace, slowly soaring over the red canopy, and Dreyden matches my speed.

"When?" I glare. "You're always gone, and you're beyond exhausted when you're home."

He was quiet for a moment as he thought over his answer. "I've been trying to give you space, and I keep my time filled by helping the people of Tartarus. That doesn't mean I don't have time for you to teach you things I'd like you to learn. Things you *need* to learn.

He always does this. He tells me what he thinks I need, but the reality is I don't *need* anything. I have everything I need. I *want* space to work through my grief, I *want* to learn to use my powers to the fullest extent, and I *want* to spend days in peace with my mate without arguing about what I *need*.

I roll my eyes toward the sky. "And what haven't I learned that you'd like me to learn? I'm flying, aren't I?" I throw my hands in the air as the volume of my voice increases. "I'm training almost every single day, aren't I? That's not good enough for you? What am I missing?"

Dreyden comes to a halt, fluttering in place. It takes me a second to stop, but I turn around to meet his hard eyes.

"Everything you do is good enough, Adeena," his voice is softer than I was expecting after I raised mine. "You are a high lady, and we don't know what exactly that entails yet. It may never mean anything more than what it is now, but what if it does? What else will we face in our lifetimes? I need you to be strong both mentally and physically if I'm going to stay sane throughout our lives."

I shake my head as I create more distance between us. "You're not hearing me." My head drops as I hold back tears. "You're not listening."

Dreyden flies closer, trying to maintain eye contact. "I'm trying to, Adeena, I really am. I'm just struggling to watch you spend so much time with Geras, yet you push me away. You say you need space, and I feel like I'm giving that to you, but I'm missing out. I wish I could have been there for your first flight. Your first everything. I want to be there for it all."

He's pulling on my heartstrings. I want to be angry, but the look on his face melts my insides. He's hurting more than he'll ever say aloud.

"You're giving me space in all the wrong ways. You disappear all week, then return exhausted and grumpy, and you bully Geras around every chance you get."

Dreyden's eyes widen at the mention of his interactions with Geras. "How do you know about that?"

I laugh in disbelief, "Geras and I are closer than you think, and harassing the poor guy only amuses him." I cross my arms over my chest. "That's beside the point, though. I'm trying to tell you I need your *support*, not your demands or disagreements."

His eyes flicker to my wings, and I know he can tell I'm tiring. "I do support you, but-"

A flash of movement in the forest below catches both of our eyes. We clamp our mouths shut, abruptly ending this conversation as we follow the movement, hovering silently over the trees.

I catch a glimpse of an unfamiliar man inside an opening in the trees. "Who is that?" I whisper as we watch him.

The man is walking quickly, but he seems disoriented and rattled by a lack of direction. Small branches tangle in his feet as he moves, nearly bringing him to the ground. He's fae, and I'm pretty sure that's the only thing keeping him upright.

Dreyden's eyes darken as he watches the man. "I don't know. I've never seen him before."

"What should we do?" I ask quietly, not wanting to unknown man to hear us.

Without warning, Dreyden descended through the trees, falling as quickly as he could before hitting the ground with a thunderous crack, one loud enough to frighten anyone passing through. Caught off guard and a slower flier than Dreyden, I took longer to reach the bottom of the forest. Maneuvering around branches and vines was tedious and hard, but the high lord made it look easy.

I land gently beside Dreyden, surveying the situation.

The unfamiliar man is tall, well built, and muscular, and he has silver eyes like mine. His faded hair is a deep burgundy, styled neatly on the top. He looks well put together, but he's clearly confused or under some sort of spell. I glance toward Dreyden, trying to read what he's thinking, but his face is expressionless.

"Who are you?" Dreyden demands the answer from the stranger.

Unsure what to say or do, the man looks Dreyden up and down, then looks toward me. He opens his mouth to speak, but quickly shuts it when Dreyden steps closer.

"Why are you here?" Dreyden's voice is growing impatient.

The man begins to shake, quivering in place as the strength of Dreyden's intimidation keeps him from finding words.

Annoyed with Dreyden's alpha personality and feeling sorry for the man, I brush Dreyden's arm, nudging him out of my way as I step closer to the man. "What is your name?" I ask, my voice gentle.

The man stops shaking as he focuses on my face, temporarily forgetting about the deadly high lord standing beside me.

"My, my name is Arryn," he forces the words out. "Who are you? Where am I?"

I feel Dreyden inhale beside me, ready to speak, but I shoot him a warning glare, shutting his mouth quickly. If we want to figure out who this man is, Dreyden needs to stay quiet.

"My name is Adeena, and you're in Fire Court. Where are you going?"

Arryn whispers my name under his breath, leaning forward and touching his chin as he goes deep in thought.

He seems lost for words once more, so I ask again, "Where are you going?"

His eyes meet mine, and I see what appears to be pain behind the silver irises. "I don't know..." he trails off deep in thought again.

Irritated, Dreyden's voice is deep beside me, "You don't know or you don't remember?"

Arryn's words are unsteady as they leave his mouth, "I... don't know." He watched Dreyden get even more agitated, forcing him to stumble through his thoughts. "I can't remember. Both. I don't know."

Dreyden and I look toward each other, unsure what is wrong with Arryn. Dreyden looks mostly annoyed, but he clearly doesn't have a clue either.

"Let's take him to a healer?" I ask Dreyden. "Maybe one of them will know what's wrong with him. It looks like a spell of some sort."

Nodding in agreement, Dreyden opens a portal.

Arryn jumps back, frightened by the inferno of flames opening out of thin air. I grab Arryn's arm with a reassuring smile.

"It's okay, Arryn. We're going to take you to one of our healers. I think you're under some sort of spell, and I want them to look at you. I need you to walk through this portal with me. It's the fastest way back to the castle."

"Castle?" he asks as he stares into the portal.

I pull on his arm, inching him closer to the opening we need to walk through. Dreyden steps behind us, ready to push Arryn through if he doesn't hurry up.

"Yes, a castle. We live there," I say as I continue to move him closer to the portal.

Dreyden steps closer, and I'm shooting him warning glares with my eyes. If he pushes Arryn through the portal I'm going to be pissed. Arryn is in a fragile state of mind right now, and he doesn't need a high lord shoving him around, even if that high lord is my mate.

Impatient as always, but more gentle than normal, Dreyden waves his hand through the air, moving the portal closer to us. We're only a step away now.

Arryn's eyes grow wider and wider as the portals nip at my back. "You can trust me," I whisper, urging him to take the final step.

Looking between the portal and me once more, Arryn sighs, "You said your name is Adeena?"

"Yes, Arryn, my name is Adeena."

He nods with Dreyden at his back, basically breathing down his throat to get going. "Okay, let's go."

Without hesitation, I tug him the rest of the way into the portal. He gasps, holding his breath like I'm pulling him underwater.

I hear Dreyden scoff as we disappear into the flames.

What's his problem?

Chapter Three

ADEENA

The Fire Court healers didn't find anything wrong with Arryn, which was disappointing, to say the least. They agreed it was possible he hit his head so hard it caused memory loss, or he's under a spell more secretive and silent than they'd seen, but they couldn't say for sure, and they didn't have a cure for him. A goblet of water and some fruit later, he was still the same: lost, confused, and scared.

"Why don't you join us for dinner, Arryn?" I ask as we are leaving the healer's office. "Fruit and water will not be enough to fill you up, and we could use the company."

Rubbing his hand over his growling stomach, Arryn says, "I don't want to intrude, but I am certainly hungry. I suppose I could join you for this one evening, but I mustn't make a habit of it."

"Dreyden will join us at dinner, but you're welcome to sit by me. Our friends Lyra and Izan will be there as well, and they're much friendlier than Dreyden."

Unsurprisingly, Dreyden had followed us into the healer's office when we arrived at the castle, but I quickly shooed him off. His sudden bad mood was ruining my good day and it was making Arryn even more nervous than he already was. I don't know what got into him, but he needs a serious attitude adjustment by the time we meet for dinner.

"Dreyden is the high lord?"

I nod, "Yes, Dreyden is the high lord, and you're in Fire Court."

"When did I get here?"

This is the fifteenth or sixteenth time Arryn has asked me this question, but I smile as I answer him, feeling bad about the extreme memory loss he is experiencing, "I'm not sure. We found you in the woods, then we brought you here. You are safe with us."

A glimmer of hope lights up Arryn's eyes as we walk. "Thank you."

"It's my pleasure. We are lucky we stumbled upon you when we did. There's no telling where you would have ended up."

Arryn rolls his shoulders back like he has a chill. "Or *who* would have found me."

I give him a reassuring smile. "I guess we'll never know."

Leading Arryn through the maze of hallways I know so well now, I give him a brief tour on the way to the dining room. He is mesmerized by the towering cathedral windows and bold décor scattered throughout the castle. His jaw is nearly dragging across the marble floor the entire way, and it only drops lower when we enter the dining room, offering him his first chance to lay eyes on Lyra.

She greets him with a gentle smile, undoubtedly having already heard all about his amnesia from the castle staff. Arryn is undeniably attractive, and I knew word of him would spread like wildfire once some of Lyra's friends caught a glimpse. A chiseled jawline complimented his broad shoulders well, and his silver eyes popped against the burgundy undertones running through his dark, lush hair. He towered over me as I stood next to him, but he wasn't as tall as Dreyden.

Lyra is seated facing us. On a normal night, she sits in the chair next to me, with Izan to her right, and Dreyden to my left. However, tonight Arryn will sit between me and Lyra because Izan and Dreyden cannot be trusted to be nice. Dreyden's poor mood always rubs off onto Izan, creating a domino effect throughout the castle, and tonight is not the night for that. Arryn needs compassion and stability while we wait for him to come out of this amnesic state.

Rising from her chair with the same grace she has always had, Lyra speaks with a pearly smile, "It's nice to meet you, Arryn. My name is Lyra Pagonis, and I'd love for you to dine with me this evening."

Silver bangles chime at Lyra's wrist as she raises her hand to her thick braid, softly twirling a loose strand between her fingers. The gown she selected for dinner was *clearly* chosen with the intention of making a lasting first impression on Arryn. Iridescent crystals line Lyra's waist, highlighting her small torso while strips of white tulle flow from her hips. The snow-white fabric only makes her deep ebony skin more gorgeous, and I notice she coated her body in a shimmery moisturizer, creating a holographic aura around her.

I grin as I look down at my attire. There wasn't time to change before dinner, and I'm still wearing the same tunic and trousers I wore all day. By now, I'm used to being outdressed by Lyra on nearly every occasion. Dressing up is Lyra's self-care and therapy.

Arryn clears his throat, silver eyes locked on the stunning woman before us. "It would be my pleasure to dine with the most beautiful women in this castle," he coolly gestures between me and Lyra.

Unexpected warmth rises to my cheeks as he charms us. I can't help but blush; Arryn is one of the most attractive men I've ever seen. His natural features are seductive and sexy, even when he looks confused. Perhaps he's our damsel in distress.

Dreyden's jealous, low growl vibrates across the dining room as he enters with Izan by his side. The attitude adjustment I had hoped for hasn't happened, causing me to roll my eyes at Dreyden.

Lyra's eyes immediately leave a startled Arryn to follow Izan across the room. There is a shift in her jade eyes that I know only I notice, a sudden twinkle as she watches Izan stride toward his place setting at the table. He glances up at her through gentle eyes but doesn't say anything as he walks.

"I wonder if it's acceptable to court another man's mate where you come from, Arryn?" Dreyden's chair scratches against the marble floor as he aggressively pulls it from the table. "It's a shame you can't remember."

Stunned by Dreyden's lack of hospitality, Arryn says nothing as he watches the high lord.

Lyra and I both shoot Dreyden a glare at the same time.

"He was only being friendly, Dreyden. There's no need to be rude to our guest," Lyra snaps at Dreyden through gritted teeth, then flashes Arryn a sweet smile.

"And I am only thinking out loud," Dreyden says as he shrugs his shoulders, then takes his place at the table.

Lyra scoffs, "Some thoughts are better kept inside your arrogant head."

A chuckle escapes my lips, catching me by surprise. I throw my hands over my mouth, covering the traitorous tongue. Lyra and Dreyden get along well enough most days, but two stubborn, outspoken individuals such as themselves are bound to butt heads.

This time it's Izan shooting me a look, silently reminding me that now is not the time to encourage Dreyden's mood to decline further than it already has. I straighten my back, then clear the shit-eating grin from my face as they continue to nitpick each other.

"One of the perks of being a high lord is the ability to speak my mind without consequence, especially within my own home." Dreyden rips into a steaming turkey leg through tightly clenched teeth.

Lyra covers her heart with her hand, gasping at Dreyden's lack of table manners. We're all staring at him, wondering what the hell got into him.

I've had enough of this.

"Shall we?" I ask the room, pointing toward the chairs. "I'm starving."

Lyra nods as she pulls her repulsed face away from Dreyden. "Me too," she says as she takes her seat.

Arryn follows me toward the table, never taking his eyes off Dreyden. He sits beside Lyra, and I sit beside him. Dreyden and Izan head the table on each end. No one sits across from us, which allows me an unobstructed view of the doors.

Thea and Revna emerge from the kitchen the second we're all seated, almost as though they were listening through the door, quietly waiting for us to take our seats. The table has a full spread of turkey, potatoes, ripe fruits, and roasted vegetables.

Revna and Thea make their way around the table, unfolding our napkins, and placing them in our laps as they greet us for dinner.

"How was your day with the high lord?" Revna asks while she raises a bottle of wine to my gold goblet.

Without a doubt she already knows all about Arryn; she would have been one of the first to find out about him. Thea and Revna know everything about this place, and everyone in it.

I smile up at the red-haired woman, thankful she continues to ask about my day when she already knows the answer. Talking to her always feels therapeutic in a motherly sort of way, and I appreciate the friendship we've formed.

"It was wonderful. We swam all morning, then went for a flight over the Bloodred Forest. It's even more devastatingly beautiful from above." I turn to Arryn beside me. "That's how we found Arryn. He's going to be staying with us for a little while. Would you mind preparing a room for him?"

Arryn hungrily shovels a mixture of turkey and potatoes into his mouth, oblivious to our conversation. He eats as though he hasn't seen food for years. Lyra's face nearly makes me laugh again when I get a glimpse of her furrowed brows and deep frown.

"You're going to get wrinkles," I lean forward, whispering to Lyra.

She straightens, trying hard to relax the muscles in her face.

Revna places her hand on the back of my chair. "There is already a room made up for him, Miss Adeena. I asked two of the girls to prepare his room as soon as you arrived. Is there anything else I can do for you?"

Of course, she already had a room made up for him. I'm not surprised in the least bit. She's always ten steps ahead of me.

Shaking my head, I offer her a smile as I say, "No, thank you. We appreciate your hard work and attention to detail."

"You're welcome, Miss Adeena. Please let me know if you find there's anything else you need done." She pats my shoulder gently as she returns to the kitchen with Thea.

We eat dinner mostly in silence. Lyra is disgusted with the way Arryn eats, Dreyden is fuming from his chair, Arryn is stuffing his face, Izan stays quiet to keep the peace, and I am unsure how to break the tension in the air.

Arryn is last to set his fork down, realizing we've all been quietly waiting for him to finish his meal. Dreyden and Izan immediately stand.

"I'm going to bed," Dreyden mumbles before stalking out of the room.

Izan gives the three of us a swift nod. "Thank you for dining with us this evening, Arryn. I'm sure we'll be seeing you tomorrow."

Arryn shyly smiles up at him, "I look forward to it."

"High lady," Izan bows slightly, lowering his eyes as he leans in my direction.

I will never get used to that.

"Goodnight, Izan. Thank you for dinner."

Raising his eyes, he looks to Lyra next. "Goodnight, Lyra."

Lyra's eyes are locked on him. "Actually," she says as she removes the napkin from her lap. "I was wondering if you'd like to join me on a walk through the garden this evening. It's too beautiful of a night to not enjoy it."

I swear I see a hint of pink flush across Izan's cheeks as he says, "I'd love to."

Lyra stands from her chair, taking Izan's outstretched hand as she rises, their eyes never leaving each other. She keeps her hand in his as they begin walking toward the doors.

She turns to look at me and Arryn as they reach the exit. "Thank you for a lovely dinner, Arryn. We look forward to seeing you again tomorrow."

"The pleasure is all mine," he beams at my drop-dead gorgeous friend.

She offers him a gentle smile. "Goodnight, Adeena. I hope Dreyden's pissy mood improves."

"Hmm," I tap my chin. "Me too. He's rather exhausting lately, isn't he?"

She laughs, "He is, indeed."

"Goodnight," I sigh, waving to her before they disappear through the doorway.

Arryn and I are all that's left. I can't explain it, but I feel protective over Arryn. We need to figure out what's going on with him and why he was in the Bloodred Forest in the first place.

We sit in silence for several seconds before Arryn turns toward me with tired eyes. "I think it's time for me to retire as well."

I couldn't agree more. The muscles in my back ache from flying for so long, and I'm ready to have a little chat with Dreyden about his attitude problem. He can't treat house guests like shit just because they're male. I don't act this way when we have female guests in the castle. It's not fair and it's immature, especially for a four-hundred-year-old high lord.

One of the castle staff members waits outside the dining room for Arryn, ready to take him to his room. We walk out together, then part ways for the evening as I leave to find my mate.

DREYDEN IS WORKING at his desk when I enter our bed chambers. Loose papers are scattered across the darkly stained wood as he scribbles notes on a pad above them. His eyes leave the desk, glancing up at me as I cross the room, walking toward him.

"What's wrong with you?" I ask as soon as I reach the opposite side of his desk, bracing my hands on the wood.

He drops the pen from his hand, crossing his arms as he leans back into his chair. This is what I call his relaxed alpha male posture. "What's wrong with me? What's wrong with him?"

I narrow my eyes at him. "He was being friendly, not a flirt. You're being unfair."

"That's not what it sounded like when I walked into the dining hall." His voice is cold.

I lean over the desk, trying to flex the brittle air between us. "You were in a horrible mood long before that. What happened?"

Dreyden sits forward, leaning closer to my face as he rubs his rough hand along his jaw. "I don't like the way he looks at you." His knee rising and falling catches my eye. He's anxiously tapping his foot against the floor. "And don't you think it's a tad suspicious that the healers couldn't find anything wrong with him, yet he says he can't remember anything? That's not weird to you?"

"Of course, it's weird to me, Dreyden. Why wouldn't it be?" I toss my hands in the air, already frustrated with how this conversation is going. "But, he hasn't given us *any* reason not to trust him, and I think he needs our help."

"He needs to find a new place to stay," Dreyden growls under his breath, his patience running thin.

"He'll stay here until he's ready to leave," I snap. "You're being ridiculous."

"I don't think I am, Adeena. I'm being cautious, and you should too." His voice is more gentle than I was expecting, considering I'd just told him he was being ridiculous.

"And I appreciate you being cautious, but something is telling me we need to help him. You know I can take care of myself and there is no need to be this protective. I'll be fine."

Dreyden rises from his chair, slowly walking around his desk until he stops behind me. He places his hands on his desk, hovering around both sides of me as I brace the wood. His woodsy-amber scent sends chills up my spine as the air around us grows heavy.

"You are my *mate,* and I *will* be protective of you. I know you don't need me to look out for you, but we both know I will go insane if I don't. It's my job to protect you. Our mating bond writes that into my brain chemistry." He presses into my body, pooling heat between my thighs.

I drop my head lower, closing my eyes as I shake it in disagreement. "Your *job* is to be the high lord."

"Mmm, maybe," he breathes without missing a beat. "But you come first."

I turn around to meet his darkening eyes. He's so close I can feel the warm exhale of each breath he releases. I can hardly concentrate, quickly forgetting the initial reason for this conversation.

"The people come first," I manage to whisper.

He closes the gap between us, forcing our noses to touch, and I can almost taste his lips on mine. "I've put my people first for the last four hundred years, and they've been well taken care of. This time is for *us*. Let us have this." His hand slips around my lower back, pulling me closer to him.

How does he do this to me? One minute I can be so irritated and angry with him, and the next he has me practically melting into the palm of his hand. Our mating bond gives me whiplash.

Or maybe it's just him.

I grip the front of his shirt, pulling him closer. My sharp fae ears pick up the faint sound of his heartbeat as it pounds harder. "You have me right now. What would you like to do with this time?" My voice is breathy and low as I press against his lips.

A wicked grin spreads across his face, igniting a fire deep within my core. He sucks his lower lip between his teeth as his eyes devour me in one look. "Mmm," he growls. "I think I'd like to have you as dessert with my after-dinner drink."

Always so quick with his words. I feel the darkness inside me push toward the surface, begging him for more. My lips twitch, turning upward as I watch him.

His free arm moves beside me, and his hand emerges from the wooden desk firmly gripping a glass full of his favorite whiskey. He swirls it under my nose, sending sweet caramel and buttery notes spiraling into my lungs. Refusing to break locked eyes, he draws the glass to his lips, then slowly swallows down a long, sexy drink of whiskey. Setting the now-empty glass on the desk behind me, he nips at my bottom lip, demanding my mouth open for him. As his tongue enters my mouth, the reminiscence of the alcohol burns my tastebuds followed by a creamy caramel flavor infused into the whiskey.

A low moan escapes me as his tongue rolls with mine, dominating my mouth. He's leaning into me with so much weight I can hardly keep myself upright, and I reach for the desk behind me to relieve the pressure. In my flustered state, I accidentally knock over his whiskey glass, sending it crashing to the floor. It explodes beside us as it connects with the marble and glass flies everywhere.

"Oops," I say, reluctantly pulling away from his firm grasp. "I'll clean it up."

"Later," he growls with intense aggression, slamming my body back into his as he purposefully moves his foot, crunching a piece of broken glass under his boot.

I can feel his massive cock swelling against me, and my voice is almost inaudible as I slowly nod, repeating his words, "Later."

A wicked grin exposes his perfectly white teeth, and a possessive moan rips from his throat as he gets excited for what's about to come.

A hint: both of us.

I reach for his belt buckle, making quick work of getting it undone while Dreyden kisses across my jaw, then down my neck. Goosebumps rise across my skin. The button on his trousers pops with ease, and I let my head drop back as the sound of his zipper sliding down reaches my ears. It's one of my favorite sounds.

My mouth waters as I slide my hand over the hard bulge begging to be released from his tightening trousers. Dreyden's throaty growl vibrates through us, egging me on harder. The heat between my thighs is becoming uncomfortable without his touch, and I'm nearly whimpering for his cock.

I lick my lips, wetting them in preparation for his stiff cock as I wiggle his trousers down. It springs free, bouncing as my mouth closes in. My tongue reaches the tip of his cock first, gently flicking over the head before my lips close around it.

"Fuck," he growls through a tightened jaw.

I keep going, bobbing my head up and down while maintaining firm pressure with my lips wrapped widely around his cock. Using my hand to stroke what my mouth can't reach, I let out a throaty moan, vibrating around his great length.

His hips jerk, but I'm ready for him as his cock hits the back of my throat, pushing so deep it nearly gags me. With animalistic instinct, Dreyden's fingers lace through my hair, then he slams his cock deeper down my throat. I part my lips as wide as my jaw will stretch while he fucks my mouth.

In what now feels like my past life I would have never allowed someone to dominate me in the way Dreyden does, but submitting to him in the bedroom gets me off more than I ever thought possible. My orgasms reach new heights as he pushes my body beyond its limits, and my dark side loves the rough sex more than anything. Perhaps that's why I push myself so hard in training.

I can't breathe but I stay calm as my oxygen runs low, trusting he'll know when to stop.

His molten eyes are locked on mine as he thrusts in and out of my sweet, submissive mouth. Just when I think I can't possibly hold out any longer, he slams into me as far as my throat will take him, then holds it for a second while I begin to struggle, gripping both of his thighs, but I never break eye contact.

"That's my good girl," he praises as he releases my hair and pulls his cock from my mouth.

Satisfied with my work, I smile up at him, wiping a mixture of saliva and precum from the corners of my lips.

Dreyden sweeps me off my feet and then twists my body away from him, bending me over his desk as he yanks my trousers down and tears open the back of my shirt, allowing it to fall onto the desk. He presses down on my lower back, forcing me to arch for him.

He drops to his knees behind me, spreading my legs as he goes. His tongue laps at my inner thighs while he grips my ass, kneading and pulling as he goes. My arousal drips down my legs, and he makes slow work of cleaning it up. He's drawing it out as long as he can, casually making his way toward my aching pussy.

"Dreyden, please," I pant as I clench my thighs around his face, needing more, and needing more *now*.

I feel his smile against my skin as I beg. "Always in such a hurry," he scolds through a husky, deep voice.

I can barely take his teasing. I try to dip, directing my pussy toward his mouth, but he holds me in place, bent over his desk as his tongue fucks my inner thighs. My body feels like it's going to implode if he doesn't touch me soon.

His hands stop their assault on my ass to spread my cheeks, giving him a front-row seat to my glistening pussy. A low growl escapes his lips as he dives in tongue first, lapping at my arousal. He uses his tongue to spread my folds, working his way up my center, eventually finding my clit. Sucking the sensitive nerves into his mouth, he rolls his tongue over it with firm, relentless pressure. His hand rubs along my wetness, gliding with ease as he moves around my entrance. He slips a finger in, and I let out a loud moan as he sinks deeper inside me. Pumping his finger in and out, he lets me adjust to his large fingers, all while his tongue continues to work my clit.

A second finger finds its way inside me, stretching me even further as he pumps. He doesn't wait more than a few seconds before inserting a third, then a fourth finger. He's practically fisting me at this point, and I'm slipping over the edge, following an orgasm into the depths of Hades.

I can hear how wet I am as he slides in and out, filling me with as much as I can take. "Oh fuck," I yell out. "I'm going to come."

He moans over my clit, sending vibrations racing through me as I grip the desk. I clamp down around his hand, coming over and over again. Stars shoot around me, and I feel the ecstasy of my orgasm lifting me into a high like no other.

As my orgasm begins to ease up, he removes his mouth from my clit, standing behind me as he lines himself up at my entrance. He wraps my hair around his hand, pulling my head away from the desk as my back arches, pressing my pussy against the head of his cock. I'm quivering in anticipation, impatiently waiting for him to sink into me.

He pulls his tunic over his head then grips his cock in one hand, sliding it up and down against my folds, teasing me until I can't take it anymore.

"Fuck me, Dreyden. Please," I beg through uneven breaths.

He responds by slamming into me, forcing me against the desk with enough force to nearly knock the wind out of me. I quickly correct my position, pressing against him as I brace myself over the wooden desk.

"How's that, baby?" Dreyden asks as he fucks me from behind.

"It's fucking perfect," I somehow manage to moan between thrusts.

Without pulling out, Dreyden grabs my right leg, hauling it onto the desk so that I'm standing on one leg with the other raised high. I feel my body adjust to this new, deeper position as he begins moving inside me again.

My leg weakens under the intense pleasure, but I force myself to remain standing for him.

Another orgasm is building, and I begin to feel that euphoric high once more as he pushes the limits of my pleasure. He's relentless, fucking me so hard I see nothing but stars around us, and I can't focus on anything but the juicy cock filling my pussy.

It slams in, then out. In, then out. Over and over again.

I begin pressing back, meeting each of his rough thrusts as he delivers them. I feel my ass cheeks bounce against him as we collide, and that makes me even more wet.

A loud groan tears from Dreyden's mouth, and I know he's getting close. His grip tightens around my hair, pulling harder as he fucks me. He's forcing me to ride the thin line between pleasure and pain, and he's doing it perfectly.

So fucking perfectly.

"Come with me," he commands as his hand leaves my hair to wrap around my throat, cutting off my airway.

The stars shine brighter, like flashing white orbs floating through my vision, and I feel blinded by them. The pleasure is so intense I feel like I might die if I don't come.

His free hand snakes around my waist, finding my clit as he thrusts. He rubs over it in tight circles, sending shivers up my arched spine.

Moan after moan slips through my lips, and I'm spiraling out of control. The sounds coming from my mouth can probably be heard well beyond the doors to our bed chambers, but in this moment I don't care. I needed this so badly.

"I'm going to come," I cry out as Dreyden pushes me farther.

His hand releases my clit as he drags me off the desk to stand upright against him, parallel to his rock-hard body. He's so deep inside me I can barely breathe, and I swear he's rearranging my internal organs with each thrust. I'm stretched to the maximum and I'm loving every second of it.

His grip around me is so tight I can't move as he fucks me as hard as he can. I scream out in pleasure as an intense orgasm rips through me.

Dreyden's thrusts slow as he finishes milking out his cock, spilling his seed down my legs as it seeps out of me. He peppers kisses down the back of my neck, sending one last wave of chills down my spine.

We're both panting through unstable, wild breaths as he holds me against him.

We needed this.

Chapter Four

DREYDEN

"You don't need to worry about me. I'll be fine, and Izan will be here in case anything happens. Please, just go." Adeena's silver eyes are more molten than normal, an easy way to determine her mood.

Adeena and I have spent a strong majority of the morning arguing back and forth about whether I should make my regular trip to Tartarus. My gut tells me I should stay and make sure Arryn's intentions here are pure, but Adeena thinks otherwise. She keeps telling me there's something inside her saying she needs to help him, but I don't really know what that means. I'm fairly certain she doesn't know what that means either.

I'm annoyed, but my voice is calm as I try to convince her, "I can take the day off and join your training session with Geras.

It's been too long since I've been to one and I'd like to see the progress you're making. Tartarus can wait."

She finishes lacing up her combat boots, then stands to face me. "No, it can't." She takes two small steps toward me before gently grabbing onto my forearms. "You love going there, so please don't stay here because of me. I'll be training the entire time anyway."

I run my fingers through my thick hair, stressed beyond belief as I try to decide what to do. Adeena will be pissed if I stay to keep an eye on Arryn, but will I be able to keep my head on straight being away from her? If something happens, will I be able to get back here in time? I don't know.

"Stop overthinking," Adeena snaps, pulling me from my head.

I glance up at her, locking eyes as she watches me. "I'm sorry," I sigh. "I would hate myself if something happened to you."

Her hand reaches up, cupping my face, and I wrap my hand around her wrist, holding her close for a moment.

"Nothing is going to happen." She leans toward my face, replacing her hand with a soft kiss. "Go," she whispers, ending the conversation without a second thought.

"Fine," I groan, closing my eyes for a moment before opening them.

I know if I don't go, I'll regret abandoning Tartarus for the day and she'll only be angry with me for staying. She needs space and independence, and maybe this is how I can give it to her... but what if something happens?

"Stop overthinking!" Adeena repeats, more agitated than before.

"Okay, okay," I throw my hands in the air, admitting defeat. "I'm going. I will be back for dinner as usual."

"Perfect," she smiles, instantaneously changing moods like we haven't been arguing all morning. "I hope you enjoy your time in Tartarus. Be safe, please."

Before she can step away I extend my arm, reaching for the back of her neck. I wrap my hand around her, then yank her forward, forcing her into the warmest, tightest hug I can. Her vanilla and jasmine scent fills the air around me, immediately easing my stress. I rub my hand along her silver hair, gently stroking it while she clings to me.

"I'll miss you," she says against my chest.

I pull back, giving her a few inches of space before kissing her forehead. "I'll miss you, too. If you need anything at all I want you to use one of the butterflies to contact me. The black ones are the fastest."

She nods, pulling away from our embrace. "I will. I'm going to be late for training and you know how Geras can be when I'm late. I'll see you tonight," she beams as she skips toward the front doors.

I follow her out, stopping at the top of the steps while she continues her way to the training field.

Izan slips through the open door behind me as soon as she's out of sight. "I'll watch over her, brother. There's no need to worry."

I sigh, knowing he's right. "It's hard letting her go." I turn to face him as my voice gets more serious, "Keep an eye on him. Make sure you know what he's doing at all times."

Izan nods, clearly agreeing with my decision to not trust this stranger in my home. "You know I will."

———

EACH TRIP to Tartarus is exhausting, but they're all worth it. The Tartarus monarchy fucked over so many good people, and all I want to do is help. Portaling to and from Tartarus uses a decent amount of my power reserve because the distance is so far, but I have more than enough power to get back and forth once each day.

"Alaric," I call out as I see my friend packing bags behind his family home.

I'm in Northford today, which is where I spend most of my time when I'm in Tartarus. It is one of the few villages still standing, and many people pass through the area when they're traveling.

The villagers were mostly killed off in the attacks when King Demir went on his rampage for a human bride, but this place holds several pick-up points for people needing supplies. They're all secret locations, only given out to those who truly need them. Alaric and I keep the drop-off points fully stocked with food, fresh water, blankets, and fresh sets of clothes for men, women, and children. They're sort of like a small shop, but everything is free.

"Dreyden," Alaric smiles widely as I come into view.

Alaric and I met shortly after the war with Tartarus concluded. I was in the area surveying the land, taking count of the casualties and damage. The devastation was overwhelming and chaotic, and in the midst of it all, I found Alaric cleaning up the mess, doing his best to pull the people of Tartarus back together. He's a commoner, a low-class human villager, but he's so much more than that. If it weren't for Alaric, the mass casualties would have been even greater. He's a hero to this fallen kingdom even if he refuses to acknowledge it. Honestly, he's too humble for his own good.

Razvan, Alaric's son, stood beside him, handing bags of rice one at a time while Alaric stuffed his drop-off bags full. He's an eight-year-old boy, but you'd never know that based on how he acts. His maturity expands beyond a boy, reaching that of a young man. The crumpling kingdom forced him to grow up, to assist his father in providing for his mother, Ellia, and his younger sister, Braylee. Razvan's dirty blonde hair is cut short on the sides with a little extra on the top, closely matching Alaric's.

"Hello, Razvan,' I greet the young man as I approach.

He grins the widest smile and has the brightest twinkle in his eyes as he sees me, reminding me he's only eight. "Hi, Dreyden. We're almost ready. Dad says that maybe I can go with you next month. Can you believe it?"

I look up, briefly making somewhat amused eye contact with Alaric. He's smiling with his eyes... always so proud of his son. We both know Razvan won't be joining us any time soon. It's too dangerous. The only reason Alaric has made it this long is because I'm here with him while we make the drop-offs. Without my protection, he would have been killed by now, likely murdered by looters or one of the escapees from the Wychwood Forest.

I play along with Alaric anyway, happy that Razvan continuously has something to look forward to while living in such dark times. "Really?" I ask as I stroll forward. "Do you think you're up for the job?"

The light in Razvan's eyes dims as his voice turns serious, "I'm definitely ready. I've been practicing my fighting skills against the bags of rice in the cellar."

I couldn't help but laugh, letting out the lightest chuckle. "I'm sure you're showing those bags of rice who's boss, am I right?"

Alaric snorts so quietly that I almost didn't catch it, and Razvan didn't catch it while he was busy staring at my gold wings shining in the morning sunlight. "I thought I walked in on a bag of rice falling on top of you while you struggled to stay upright, but I could have been seeing things."

Razvan stared blankly at his father, at a complete loss for words.

"I'm sure you were seeing things," I say, shooting Razvan a reassuring look.

The young man-boy's light returns to his eyes. "Yeah, that's definitely it." A sly, mischievous smile spreads across his young face.

Snapping my fingers, the pocket portal carrying my supplies opens beside me, widening Razvan's eyes so much they look like they'll pop out of his little head. He does this every time. "I brought more blankets, beans, and seasonings."

Seasonings are an extremely rare luxury in Tartarus during this time, and they may not be needed, but I know they provide a sense of home when they're used. The people of Tartarus are fighting for their lives, eating what they can, when they can, and most of the time that doesn't include any type of seasoning in their food. Plain old rice and beans. Spices remind them of simpler times when food wasn't so scarce or difficult to hold onto once they had it.

"What kind of seasonings?" Ellia says as she exits the house.

Her long brown hair is braided behind her back, resting over her floral dress. Dark circles dim her blue eyes, and I can feel her exhaustion from across the yard.

"Hello, Ellia," I say with a quick wave and a nod. "There's a mixture of spices in the bag today. Revna found what she could in the market and brought it back for us. I saw cinnamon, clove, and pepper. I'm not sure what else is in there, but you're welcome to look through it."

"I think I will," she beams as she pulls the bag from the portal. "I've had a craving for cinnamon toast."

Ellia's stomach is round and swollen with a growing child inside. It doesn't look like it'll be much longer before the baby arrives. This child is a blessing from the gods, but I'm scared for her. I'm scared for all of them. Childbirth in Tartarus with no clinics or healers will be scary. I've offered to let them stay in Fire Court when the time comes, but they declined. Their mission here is their top priority, and they know there's no one to take their place supplying the drop-off locations. I could do it myself, but it would take even more time and I don't have the connections to spread the word like Alaric does. His network spreads far beyond my knowledge of the area.

A toddler, barely able to walk, emerges from the doorway. Platinum blonde curls top her head, bouncing as she toddles her way into the yard. "Mmm... ma-ma," she says in the tiniest little voice.

"Come here, Braylee," Ellia calls to her as she shuffles through the bag of spices, eventually finding a small container of cinnamon.

Braylee giggles at her mother's voice. Razvan meets her halfway, grabbing her hand as he gently leads her toward Ellia.

Alaric rises from his squatting position, throwing a heavy bag over his back, then raises two more from the ground.

I empty my pocket portal one bag at a time, filling the cart we use to transport supplies. Keeping the supplies in my pocket portal would be ideal, but I don't have enough power reserves to hold everything while I'm here and portal back to Fire Court at the end of the day. It's too risky, especially when I must fight feral creatures and looters nearly every day.

Traveling with supplies in the open like this draws attention, but it's what we must do if we want to continue making large drop-offs at several locations.

"Ready to head out?" Alaric asks when I've finished loading the cart.

"Yes, are you?"

"I'm as ready as I'll ever be," he sighs, knowing the day ahead will be long. It's already brutally hot outside, and it's only going to get worse.

Ellia scoops Braylee out of the grass, carrying her on her hip as she walks toward Alaric. "Be safe out there. It's getting worse."

"Always am," Alaric smiles, planting a soft kiss on his wife's forehead.

Her eyes close at his gentle touch, and I wonder if this is the human equivalent of fated mates. Alaric and Ellia share a soft, sweet love that I've only seen a few times throughout my life. He puts Ellia and their children first, day after day, and night after night. His love for his family is admirable, and it makes me hopeful for my future with Adeena.

Ellia turns toward me like she does every morning. "Keep him safe," she threatens through worried eyes.

I cross my hand over my chest, covering my heart. "With my life."

Razvan grabs onto his father, hugging him for dear life before reluctantly letting go. "I love you, Dad," he says as he holds back sad tears.

We do this every morning, and you'd think I'd be used to it by now, but I'm not, and it chokes me up every time. It breaks a small piece of my heart watching Alaric say goodbye to his family like it'll be the last time. If anything were to happen to Alaric on my watch, I could never forgive myself.

"Time to go," Alaric announces as he steps away from Ellia, kissing her hand before turning to leave.

Oh, my heart. Perhaps I should start kissing Adeena's hand before parting ways. It's such an intimate, loyal gesture.

Alaric and I sneak our way around the ghost town of North-ford, slipping into four different drop-off locations throughout the day. It's obvious that word of the secret drop-off locations has become more widespread because they were all nearly depleted of their resources. Our daily supply drops aren't enough for the starving families of Tartarus. I can't carry more in my pocket portal from Fire Court, so I don't know how to fix this problem.

Tartarus is not self-sufficient right now because of looters. They steal anything and everything they can get their hands on, and that includes crops. Toward the beginning of summer, some of the locals planted fields of vegetable gardens in an attempt to be more self-sustaining. That dream was quickly squashed when looters rampaged through the fields, destroying every single plant. They did it for sport, for fun. I felt physi-cally ill over it after watching how hard the locals worked to get the fields prepped and planted. I still feel sick over it.

We wrap up the hot, exhausting day and make our way back into the streets, quietly rolling the empty cart behind us. Alaric and I don't speak while we walk to keep our known presence to a minimum.

We're nearly back to Alaric's family home when we cross paths with a father and small child, no more than three years old. I haven't seen them before, so I assume they're new to town. The child holds her father's hand as they walk, and it's not hard to tell she's struggling to keep up. He walks slowly, unsteady on his feet as they cross the gravel road. My heart sinks to the pit of my stomach knowing that if they were attacked, this father would be defenseless and unable to keep this child safe. They'll be killed immediately if they're caught in the open.

As they come closer, I realize how visible the child's ribs are. She's wearing a pink dress, and it would be fit for the small princess I'm sure she is if it wasn't tattered and torn. Her soft brown hair is ratted all the way to her scalp, and I can only imagine how long it has been since she has had a brush run through her beautiful locks.

The child's father is in bad shape as well, worse off than her. He likely hasn't eaten far longer than her. He looks close to death with his recessed eye sockets, holding no muscle at all in his face. His arms and legs are depleted of all fat, and he reminds me of a walking skeleton.

I need to find a way to bring more food into the area and keep these people safe from the dark creatures destroying this kingdom. It'll be next to impossible on my own, but I must find a way.

I hate myself for nearly staying in Fire Court this morning. I need to do better.

Chapter Five

DREYDEN

I'm deep in thought and my mind feels clouded as I arrive back in Fire Court, so I take a short walk through the woods to decompress before going inside for dinner.

There are so many wonderful things to be grateful for here in Fire Court, and I wish I could share it all with the people of Tartarus without making my people suffer in return. We don't have enough resources to spread across both lands, and even if I did, that doesn't solve the looter and feral creature problem. It's going to take a lot more than I can do on my own, but with the other courts turning their back on Tartarus, I don't know where to begin. For once in my life, I'm truly stumped. I'm at a loss for what to do.

Fireflies light my way, dancing around me as I emerge from the woods onto the training field. It's dark, but with fae eyesight, I can see better than a human. My ears pick up on male voices as I step farther into the field. I can't see the other side, but I can hear people talking.

My senses send me on high alert, and I prepare for what I'm walking into.

The unfamiliar voices get louder as I stalk across the field, ready for a fight. I hear three *male* voices, and I don't like that shit.

My blood is already boiling and I'm angry as their outlines form in my vision. They appear smaller than I am, but definitely fae. They're standing in a circle, speaking inaudible words.

Light flickering inside the castle catches my eye, and that's when I notice the castle is more lit up than normal. The candles are lit in every room on the guest wing.

Strange...

I can see them, but they haven't seen me yet, which allows me to take a closer look before approaching. They're standing awkwardly, not in a way I would expect three male travelers to hold a conversation.

I inch closer.

"You knock first," the shortest man snaps at the tallest man. "You're the biggest."

"That's not fair! I don't even know where we are. They could be standing behind the door waiting to kill me for all I know.

I'm not doing it," he responds, the frustration growing in his voice.

The third man stands between them, silently watching them argue.

"Well, *someone* has to do it, and it's not going to be me," the shortest man snorts as he crosses his arms.

Both men turn toward the man between them, setting their sights on him.

He shakes his head back and forth as he raises his hands in defense, "No. I'm not doing it. I'll sleep on this field tonight before knocking on a stranger's door at night."

Having enough of their roundabout conversation, I step forward, revealing myself as I light fire between my fingertips. "No one will be sleeping in my training field, I'm afraid," I announce as I cross the grass, stalking toward them.

The three men freeze in place, clamping their mouths shut at the sound of my voice. Their eyes bulge from their heads, widening when they see the flames illuminating my hands.

"Who are you, and why are you here?" I ask as I close in.

The shortest one speaks up first, "I-I don't know. We don't know why we're here."

My flames grow hotter, expanding in size as my temper shortens. "What do you mean you don't know?" I bark.

He jumps, nearly falling backward as my deep voice assaults his eardrums. Words don't leave his mouth as he quivers, shaking his head while closing his eyes.

He can pretend I'm not here, but that'll only get him into more trouble.

I turn toward the taller man, glaring at him while I wait for someone to answer.

Cracking to the pressure, the tall man's voice is unsteady as he speaks, "We truly don't know, sir. We-"

"High Lord," I growl, cutting him off as I correct him.

"High Lord," he quickly repeats, swallowing his fear. "We all arrived in this field at the same time, and we don't know why. We're all lost."

My mind snaps back to Arryn, the lost traveler Adeena decided to keep as a house pet. He had said he was lost... and now these three men are lost in my field.

The third man clears his throat. "We don't know where we are. We were going to knock on the castle doors, but we hesitated because it was late and we didn't know who lived here." He eyes me up and down, visibly terrified and regretting being here.

I watch the three of them for a moment, scanning them repeatedly as I attempt to decide what to do. I can't leave them out here in the field. I could kill them for trespassing, but I don't think Adeena would be very happy with me, and they could be telling the truth...

I roll my eyes to the back of my head, letting out a long sigh. "You may stay here for one night, and one night only. You will leave at first daylight."

The smallest man clasps his hands together like he's praying to the gods. "Oh, thank you, sir!"

"High lord!" the tallest man corrects him immediately, then looks to me. The fear in his eyes tells me he's looking to see if I'm going to decapitate him right here and now for misuse of my title.

"Right, my apologies. Thank you, High Lord," the smallest man says apologetically.

The other two nod and thank me in unison.

A wicked smile crosses my lips. "You're just in time for dinner. Follow me." I turn toward the castle, waving them on as I begin to walk. "We're going to be late if you don't hurry up. You've wasted enough of my time already."

I'm being cold with them, but I don't care. I don't like this one bit. First, Arryn shows up in my forest, supposedly lost and confused, and now these three dumbasses are here arguing in my training field. It's suspicious.

One night, then they're gone.

The three dumbasses follow me inside, keeping a safe distance from my flaming hands, but following close enough to annoy me. We scale the stairs leading to the front entrance to the castle. I open the doors using my power, asserting even more dominance.

I lead them down the hallways while they walk in silence. The loud sound of chatter fills my ears as we get closer to the dining hall. I hear Adeena's sweet laughter, immediately easing some of my tension.

Once again, I don't recognize some of the voices I'm hearing, and it sounds like there are enough people to fill the entire room...

I turn the corner, abruptly stepping into the dining hall.

The room goes silent as I stand there, taking in everything going on.

All eyes fall to my flaming hands, and while I want to stoke the flames, growing them larger and hotter, I choose to put them out instead. The look Adeena is giving me is enough to make me behave.

Adeena rises from her chair, changing the deadly glare into a soft smile as she says, "You're a little late, and I decided we shouldn't keep this many people waiting." She gestures to the table full of people.

Izan, Lyra, Adeena, and Arryn are at the table, accompanied by a shit load of strangers.

Adeena clears her throat, drawing my attention off the strangers and back to her beautiful face. "While you were in Tartarus today, we had ten more travelers show up. They're all unsure where they are or *why* they're here, but they trickled in throughout the day. They've each had rooms prepared for the evening."

I've had a long day, and everything inside me wants to fight Adeena over allowing these strangers into our home, but I've been humbled by the day I had and the things I saw, and I don't want to argue with the love of my life right now. I want a happy dinner filled with appreciation for what we have.

Tomorrow we can have this discussion.

I watch my mate through tired eyes. "I found three more on the training field on my way in. I invited them inside for dinner and told them we would make accommodations for them tonight. Are there enough guest rooms left?"

An adoring, pleased smile spread across her lips. "We might need to double up a couple of rooms, but I think we can make it work. Come sit for dinner. Revna and Thea made plenty of food."

Fourteen strangers in my home.

———

THE FOLLOWING MORNING, I wake with Adeena wrapped in my arms and Izan pounding on the door to our bed chambers.

"Wake up!" he shouts from outside the locked doors.

Adeena and I both groan, wishing he'd just go away. Gentle moments like this are what I live for, and he's fucking it up.

"If you don't get your asses out of bed right now, I'm going to knock this door off its hinges," he threatens from the other side of the door.

"Oh, he's pissed," I whisper to Adeena as I squeeze her naked body closer to mine.

"You better get the door," she giggles as I release her, rising out of bed.

My body is stiff as I pad across the cool marble floors. Depleting my power reserves really does a number on my body, and most mornings feel like a hangover because of it.

Izan's pounding increases in speed and force, and I swear he's about to hammer a hole into the door.

"I'm coming!" I snap loud enough for him to hear me. This better be worth it.

The pounding immediately stops.

I reach the door, quickly unlocking it then twisting the handle so hard I nearly break it. "What?"

Izan looks somewhat frantic, which is extremely out of character for my relaxed second-in-command. "A dozen more travelers are waiting outside the castle doors this morning."

"A dozen?" Adeena asks, shooting out of bed.

I nearly slam the door into Izan's nose as I hide Adeena's naked body from Izan's view. "You're naked!" I yell at her, scolding her sexy ass for showing Izan what's mine.

"I don't care," she snaps back. "I need to get out there."

She begins rifling through her armoire, frantically searching for her normal attire. A black tunic and black trousers, just like me.

I open the door once more for Izan once she's fully clothed and lacing up her boots. "Let me guess," I sigh, running my fingers through my hair. "They're lost and confused?"

Izan nods. "Yes. They all have the same story as the travelers who arrived yesterday."

"I don't know what to do with all these people," I say as I throw my hands in the air, suddenly remembering I'm standing in the doorway naked as well. "I'll be out there in a minute."

"See you outside," Izan says in his serious second-in-command voice as he turns to leave.

I close the door, then cross the room to get dressed. Adeena already has clothes waiting for me when I get there. She smiles up at me through sterling eyes while she hands me the pile of black fabric.

"Thank you," I say as I kiss the top of her head.

"You're welcome," she grins. "Hurry up and get dressed so we can go out there. I need to see what's going on."

Shocked she's actually going to wait for me, I quickly dress in all-black attire to match Adeena, then we make our way outside.

We're instantly overwhelmed as we step through the front entrance.

Izan wasn't wrong when he said a dozen travelers were waiting for us outside. They're all babbling and confused, asking each other questions none of them seem to have the answers to. It'd be almost comical if this wasn't happening on my land, at my home.

"I've asked the legion to begin setting up the legion camps to hold all these people. There are too many to keep in the castle, and I'm not sure we want all these strangers roaming the castle unsupervised." Izan eyes Adeena, waiting for her reaction to her plan, which is ironic considering I'm the high lord, but she does have me wrapped around her finger.

What Adeena wants, Adeena gets.

I hold my breath as I watch for her response beside him. I think this is a brilliant plan. We can't release these people onto my lands, and we have no idea what they're capable of or what their ulterior motive is.

"I think it's a good idea," Adeena agrees.

Thank the gods.

"We can keep an eye on them out here until they get their memory back or we figure out what's going on with them. They'll be safe in the camps, and they won't overrun the inside of the castle. We can run it like a normal legion camp."

"I was hoping you'd say that," Izan says, releasing the breath he was holding. The breath we were *both* holding.

"What can we help with?" she asks with more enthusiasm than I would as she steps toward the edge of the stairs.

The sunlight hits her perfectly, and the world seems to fade out around me as I focus on nothing but my beautiful mate standing before me. She's the most cheerful and passionate person I've ever met, and she's all mine.

Chapter Six

ADEENA

Puffy red eyes stare back at me in the mirror.

I spent half the morning assisting the legion in setting up the legion camp for the lost travelers. We worked quickly, distributing sleeping cots, blankets, and basic hygiene kits as soon as the tents were constructed. Every lost traveler pitched in, carrying their own weight and earning their keep.

They were hard-working and efficient as they worked alongside the legion. It's hard to tell how old they are because of how fae age, and none of them know the answer anyway. They know their names, and that is the extent of their memory.

I was stopped dead in my tracks when I turned a corner in the middle of the tents. The hygiene kits I'd been carrying fell from my hands as I froze, calling attention my way as they crashed into the ground.

Tears rose to my eyes and a ball closed off my airway, making it nearly impossible to breathe. I stood there in silence and absolute shock as I stared at the man working alongside the legion.

Arden, I thought to myself.

As I was stuck in place, unable to move, I watched the young man distribute blankets to a line of patiently waiting lost fae. Everything about him moved and looked like Arden, my brother.

Pulling myself from the trance I was stuck in, I stumbled as I took a step forward.

The man heard my foot stomp in the grass as I caught myself, and he turned to look at me.

Dread and disappointment tore through me as I made eye contact with him. It wasn't Arden. How could it have been? He was dead, lost to the Tartarus monarchy too many months ago.

Silver eyes pierced my soul as he walked toward me, once again frozen to where I stood. I couldn't move as memories of my older brother flooded my memory, taking over every corner of my mind.

"Are you okay?" he asked as he reached for my arm.

I defensively pulled away from his grip. "I'm fine," I said as I snapped out of shock.

A flood of tears was coming faster than I could control, and I turned to run inside.

And that's how I ended up here: locked in my bathing chambers, bawling my eyes out as I am overwhelmed with thoughts of my brother.

My dead brother.

Tears well in my eyes as I fight to hold them back. I need to stop crying. I need to pull myself together and get back out there to help the lost travelers. They need my help, and I shouldn't be hiding away in here crying over my brother who died nearly a year ago.

A soft knock on the door makes me jump, dragging my eyes away from the reflection in the mirror.

"Miss Adeena?" Revna's soft voice travels through the door.

I inhale deeply, sucking in my trauma as I breathe. "Yes?" I manage to say barely above a whisper.

"Is there anything I can get for you?"

Revna knows I don't need anything, but she has made a habit of knowing the exact moment I begin trying to pull myself together after a mental breakdown. It happens almost daily, but I do my best to hide it, especially from Dreyden. He already worries about me enough to drive any sane person crazy, and he has enough going on in Tartarus.

"No, thank you, Revna. I'm fine. I'll be out in a minute."

"I've left a chocolate muffin on the table for you. You haven't eaten all day and I thought you'd enjoy one of my muffins."

I smile through wet eyes, looking down at my hands braced against the countertop. Revna is so thoughtful, and I don't deserve her motherly comfort. She keeps me fed and tries her best to pick me back up after I've had a breakdown, but I always lock the door behind me so that no one can get in. Neither of us speaks of my unstable mental state, but I know she worries.

Pushing through my shaky voice, I say, "Thank you. I'll be out soon."

"Let me know if there's anything else I can get for you, Miss Adeena." I hear Revna's hand slide from where it rested followed by the click over her short heels as she exits my bed chambers.

I sigh in relief as soon as I hear the door shut behind her, falling to the floor as my back slides down the cabinets behind me. A few deep breaths do me good as I hold my hands over my face, covering the outside world.

I can do this.

I can get up. I can pull myself together and get back out there.

I have to. These people need help, and I'm feeling a pull almost as strong as my mating bond to help them. It feels like it's written in my destiny to protect these lost travelers... like they're *mine*.

Rising to my feet, I quickly find a soft towel to dip in water. A cold compress on my puffy eyes will help the swelling and redness, dissolving evidence of my mental breakdown. I'll just need to avoid Dreyden for a little while, which will be next to impossible.

The ice-cold water takes my breath away as I press it to my face, making my teeth chatter for a few seconds before my body adjusts to the frigid towel. It feels nice against my skin, almost instantly reducing the swelling in my eyes.

I can't wait for a time when I don't cry my eyes out every day, where I can live free of my trauma and embrace my past. I know it builds character, and I know it makes me who I am, but it's hard. Losing my entire family and village has been devastating to my mental health. I work through it one day at a time, and I know I'm making progress, but it's slow progress.

Once I'm semi-satisfied with the relaxed state of my eyes, I leave the bathing chambers and make my way back outside to help the legion and travelers.

I just need to avoid Dreyden.

The sun is shining brightly, and it nearly blinds me as I step into the morning light. It takes a minute for my eyes to adjust to the rays of sunlight assaulting my tired eyes, but eventually, I see the progress the legion has made since I've been inside.

They're nearly done now, and the lost travelers are settling into their tents.

The field is covered in forest-green tents. We constructed more than we needed in anticipation of more travelers. I don't know how many will show up, or why, but something tells me we're in for something big.

Dreyden was extremely reluctant to set up extra tents. He was worried the travelers would feel too "at home" and wear out their welcome, but I like to be prepared. After a quick conversation earlier this morning, Dreyden agreed to over-preparation as opposed to under-preparation. I couldn't help but smile as I won the disagreement.

Never in a million years did I think I would win an argument with the deadly high lord of Fire Court.

Yet, here I am, mated to the "deadly" man himself.

I make my way into the field, in search of something to do. There has to be at least one person who needs my help.

Izan is the first face I recognize, and I immediately turn away from him, heading in a completely different direction as I avoid eye contact. If he sees that I've been crying he'll run straight to Dreyden. So, now I need to avoid *two* people this morning.

I look behind me as I walk away from Izan to be sure he hasn't seen me and isn't following.

The open row between tents is clear, and Izan is nowhere to be found.

Safe.

As I twist my body back to face forward, I slam into a rock-hard wall.

A Dreyden-sized wall.

"Fuck," I mutter under my breath as soon as I realize it's him.

"What?" he asks, confused as I refuse to look at him. "What's wrong?" His voice is full of concern as he reaches for my chin, dragging my face to meet his.

He inhales deeply, then exhales slowly as he takes in my blood-shot eyes and puffy skin. Immediately pulling me into his warm embrace, he chooses to not push me for answers as he holds me. He doesn't know the exact reason as to why I've been crying, but he can feel my hurting heart.

Breaking our silence, I take a step back. My body feels cold as it leaves his. "When are you leaving for Tartarus? It's getting late in the morning and I'm sure Alaric will be wondering where you are."

He gives me a quick once over, probably checking to make sure I'm still in one piece like he always does. "I'm not going this morning."

"Why not?"

He *always* goes. Why wouldn't he be going? Last night before we fell asleep, he told me about a starving child and how he needs to do more, but this morning he's not going.

"I'd rather spend the day with you."

Liar.

I can tell by the way he breaks eye contact when he says it.

"Last night you sounded so sure you'd be in Tartarus as soon as the sun rose. What changed?"

He looks away again, mulling over his answer. Lying to me is not his specialty. "You look like you could use my help this morning," he says as he swipes his thumb across my cheek, staring into my still-red eyes.

I shake my head, brushing his hand off my face. "Tell me the truth or don't talk to me at all. Don't lie to my face like it's nothing." My voice is cold as I snap at him.

He looks taken aback by my lack of patience with him this morning, and I can't really blame him, but why does he have to fucking lie to me? To my face.

"I'm sorry," he apologizes before I lose my temper more. "I was watching you with some of the lost travelers this morning, and I must admit I don't like the way they look at you. They're watching you like you're something to eat. They're being creeps."

I furrow my brows at him, already losing my cool. "Do you think I don't know how to take care of myself?"

"That's not what I'm saying at all. I don't trust these... people," he says as he looks around, pointing to the lost travelers.

"It sounds like that's *exactly* what you're saying." I take another step back as my rage grows. I never used to get angry this quickly with him, but he can't seem to give me a break. He's constantly pushing me, "protecting" me. I'm being smothered by his over-protective alpha male ego, and I'm sick of it. "And these people have done nothing to break our trust."

"They've done nothing to *earn* my trust, Adeena," he bites out. "Why can't you see that?"

I have nothing but nasty and mean words I'll regret, so I hold both my breath and my tongue. He watches me, waiting for my response.

Closing my eyes softly, I say, "Please, just go to Tartarus. You're not needed here today. We'll be better off without you."

I open my eyes to see the hurt penetrating his soul. My words hurt, but I chose them over a million other nasty things I could have said. A heated argument isn't what either of us needs this morning.

"You don't mean that," he says at a near-whisper.

The words are hard to form. "I *do* mean it, Dreyden. I feel pulled to help them, and you're not understanding that."

He throws his hands in the air. "How do you expect me to understand that when you won't elaborate on what it means? Do you realize how crazy you sound?"

76

Now he's being hurtful, and it doesn't feel fair. "I need you to trust me, and to not question my choices. Calling me 'crazy' is insulting and rude, and now you'd be wise to spend your day in Tartarus. I don't want to see you until dinner."

Okay, now we're both saying hurtful things, but I don't deserve this. I'm trying to follow this pull I'm feeling and help these lost travelers, and he's calling me crazy instead. I haven't lost my mind; I'm following my heart. If he can't see that... then I don't know. I don't know what that means for us.

"You're being ridiculous," he says as his eyes darken. His frustration is rising to the surface. "You can't ignore me all day."

Without missing a beat, I give him the most serious look I can. "I can, and I will. Leave me alone."

I turn to leave, but he grabs my arm before I can get more than a step away.

"You can't be serious," he scoffs in disbelief.

"Leave. Me. Alone," I scowl as I tear my arm from his grasp, storming away without looking back.

Who does he think he is?

Chapter Seven

DREYDEN

Flames rip from my palms as I lose my shit. My skin feels like wildfire as the heat rages through me.

I didn't want to leave Adeena with all those strangers this morning, but she made it clear she doesn't need me. She doesn't want me.

As soon as she tore from my grasp, leaving me standing alone between the legion tents, I opened a portal. I had to get out of there. I couldn't stay somewhere that I wasn't wanted when it felt like my mate was rejecting me.

My portal got me here in a matter of seconds. I've been standing at the edge of the forest for at least ten minutes, and my blood hasn't stopped boiling.

Today is going to be a fucking terrible day. I can feel it.

I make my way toward Alaric's family home just like every other morning, but today I'm later than normal. I hadn't planned on traveling to Northford today because of my gut feeling, but here I am, fighting against instinct.

I grunt through each step as I walk, trying to work through the extreme anger I'm feeling. I need to calm down before I get to Alaric's house. I can't let Razvan see me like this. It'll frighten him and he'll be afraid of me.

Shaking my palms, I will the flames to go out, and they reluctantly recede into my skin.

I try to loosen my stride as I stalk toward the house, but it feels next to impossible.

Adeena doesn't want my protection, and that pains me more than most of the trauma I've experienced throughout my lifetime. It's etched into my brain to protect her. How could she not want it?

Razvan appears on the horizon ahead, and I send him the friendliest wave I can as my eyes focus on him.

He's waving back with both arms, which is something I've never seen him do.

My ears begin to pick up frantic cries for help as I get within hearing range of Razvan. His face comes into focus, and his eyes are opened wider than I thought possible. That's when I realize he's not greeting me with a wave, he's trying to flag me down, panicking as he tries to get my attention. All the anger I'd been previously feeling melts away as worry settles in.

Gold wings explode from my back as reality sets in. Something's wrong. Razvan is alone in the yard, and Alaric is nowhere to be seen. I squat into a low stance, then launch my body off the ground. I soar through the sky, reaching Razvan in a matter of seconds.

"What's wrong?" I ask more assertively than I meant to.

Razvan's young man-boy face is frightened. "It's my dad! They attacked him!"

"Who attacked him?" I ask as I look around for potential threats. "Where is he?"

He points toward the house. "He's inside with Mother! He's bleeding! Mother told me to watch for you outside." His young voice is full of adrenaline.

Perhaps I was reading my gut feeling wrong this morning. Maybe this is where I was supposed to be.

I curse under my breath, scolding myself as I run inside the house with Razvan hot on my heels. I burst through their door, searching for Alaric.

My eyes meet Ellia first. She's leaning over Alaric's bloodied, beaten body while she applies pressure to a gushing wound. "Where have you been?" she screams, her voice full of anger and rage.

Ignoring her question, I cross the room toward Alaric. By the looks of it, he was attacked by looters. His body is bruised badly, and there are too many knife wounds to count. Ellia already removed most of his clothing, exposing the deep cuts. He's losing blood too quickly.

Dropping to my knees beside Alaric, I raise my hand over his body, holding it flat as I call my magic to the surface. I've used my healing powers only a handful of times. It drains my power reserves to next to nothing, but I must save my friend.

It's my fault I didn't get here sooner. This wouldn't have happened if I hadn't chosen to stay in Fire Court, hovering over Adeena and arguing about stupid shit.

Warmth spreads across my palm as magic rises to the surface of my skin. A golden aura illuminates the dim space around us as I begin moving my hand over his body.

"It's too late," Ellia cries beside me. "You're too late."

"I'm going to try," I say as I concentrate on my friend's wounds, not breaking focus as the magic spreads across his body. "He's a fighter. You know that."

Ellia goes quiet as she sobs beside me. Razvan is carrying Braylee around their little house, trying to keep her occupied and happy. He knew exactly what his mother needed.

Gold dust rises from Alaric's body, swirling around his wounds as the magic spreads. I can feel my power reserves nearing empty, but I push on.

I focus on the deepest, most obvious wounds first. The cuts on his chest stop bleeding and then begin to close. I think he'll live if the blood loss isn't too much. He's healing quickly, but human bodies are so much more frail than fae, and that makes his odds unfavorable.

Ellia folds her hand over Alaric's wrist, checking for a pulse. Her eyes widen, raising to meet mine. "It's working. His heart is getting stronger."

I sigh in relief, closing my eyes for a brief second while I try to maintain control over my healing power. My power reserves are almost dry, and I'm having a hard time staying awake.

I must save my friend.

"Dreyden, that's enough," Ellia nudges my hand as I begin to lose consciousness. "Dreyden," she repeats.

"Just a little more," I whisper through tired lips.

"He's going to live. You need to stop, Dreyden. You're hurting yourself."

Still, I continue to empty every drop of my power into him. This is my fault, and I can't have him in pain because of me.

"Dreyden!" she shouts, but her voice is lost to the void of blackness I've slipped into.

A RAGING headache pounds through my head, extending down my neck and spine. I feel like I've been thrown off the Fire Court cliffs while blackout drunk. It's comparable to a wild night out and the killer hangover that follows the next morning, but at least ten times worse.

I raise my hand to my head, covering my eyes from the candlelight beside me.

"He's awake," I hear Ellia's words from across the room.

Little hands grip my arm before I hear his young man-boy voice, "You saved him."

I remove my hand from my eyes to see Razvan kneeling beside me. The room is dark around us, only lit by candlelight. Reality floods back to me as memories of the day clear from my foggy head.

"Where is he?" I gasp as I sit up.

I must have fallen asleep after healing Alaric. How Ellia moved me across the room to this cot on the floor, I'll never know. Maybe Razvan is stronger than I've given him credit for.

"I'm fine," Alaric snaps from his matching cot across the room.

"You're not fine," Ellia scolds. "Neither of you are fine."

Alaric laughs through a painful cough, "I'm alive, aren't I?"

"I feel great," I groan as I try to stand, but I fail as I fall back onto the cot. My muscles are too weak to stand and I'm too dizzy to see straight. I look around me, realizing how dark it is outside. "I need to get back to Fire Court. Adeena must be worried sick."

Or, maybe not. She's the one who told me to leave. She said I wasn't needed there.

Ellia hands me a glass of fresh water as I find my balance in a sitting position. "You won't be going anywhere tonight. You're too weak to travel and after draining your power reserves like that, I doubt you could portal home even if you tried."

I groan at both my headache and my frustration. Ellia is right. I can feel how depleted my power reserves are, even after sleeping off most of the day. I'm too weak to stand up. There's no way I'll be able to open a portal tonight.

My only option is to stay in Northford with Alaric and his family tonight. Adeena likely won't even notice I'm gone, and if she does, she won't care.

I hate myself for reading my gut feeling incorrectly. If I'd been here early this morning none of this would have happened. Alaric would have been safe under my protection and his family wouldn't be traumatized by his near-death experience.

"What happened?" I ask, watching Alaric from across the room.

"I waited for you, but after you didn't show I decided to make rounds by myself. With the supply locations being nearly empty yesterday morning I knew I had to risk it. That little girl we saw in the street doesn't have many more days without food... and I know she's not the only one. I had to go."

It really is all my fault. He'd waited, but I hadn't shown. I'd failed not only my friend but the people of Tartarus in their time of need. Visions of the starving girl in the tattered pink dress flood my head, and I feel nauseated by my decision to spend the morning in Fire Court. I'd failed a child.

The regret in my voice is clear as I apologize to Alaric. "I'm so sorry. I had a gut feeling something was wrong today, but I thought it was going to be in Fire Court. We have 'lost' travelers showing up in groups, and they're acting weird around Adeena. I thought she was in danger, but I read it all wrong and it was you in danger. I should have been here." My eyes leave Alaric to find Ellia. "I'm so sorry," I say as we make eye contact.

Regret builds a boulder in the pit of my stomach as I sit there, watching Alaric's beautiful family. I'd nearly destroyed this family with my selfishness. Ellia is heavily pregnant, nearly ready to birth a child, yet she's exhausting herself as she takes care of me and Alaric. It should be *us* waiting on her hand on foot, not the other way around.

"You both need to take the day off tomorrow," Ellia says to both of us as she rubs her round, tired belly. "You can return to Fire Court in the morning when your strength has improved. I made a hearty stew while you were sleeping. It'll heal you right up."

Handing me a bowl of rich stew, Ellia shoots me a warning glare, silently threatening me if I try to leave. I'm not going anywhere tonight. This is where I need to be.

The bowl of stew feels warm in my hands. Carrots and potatoes float around the thick broth, steaming alongside the chunky cuts of beef. "It looks great. Thank you."

"You're welcome. Now quit talking and eat up. You look exhausted."

And I feel it. I've never drained my power reserves that low, and now I know why. Alaric is worth every painful second of it, though. Without my friend, Tartarus would fall deeper into darkness, and I'm not sure how I'd survive knowing this family lost its father.

After downing two huge bowls of stew, I'm feeling much better but ready to fall asleep for the night. Alaric made it through three-fourths of his bowl before falling asleep. Ellia was annoyed, but we both knew he needed to rest. Humans heal at a snail's pace compared to fae, and Alaric has an extensive amount of healing to do even with my intervention.

"If you ever do that to him again, I'll never forgive you." Ellia's voice is calm but cold at the same time as she rocks in a chair, nursing Braylee to sleep.

"I won't. You have my word," I speak quietly, trying to not disturb Braylee as she drifts into a world of dreams. A better world.

Chapter Eight

ADEENA

Today went smoother than I could have hoped for, and I couldn't be happier about it. Without Dreyden breathing down my neck, I was able to get so much done. The legion camp is fully set up, complete with housing tents, an outdoor kitchen, a dining room in one of the largest tents, and several washrooms. I've directed some of the castle staff to assist the lost travelers with laundry.

The lost travelers worked tirelessly alongside the legion to be prepared by nightfall. We took breaks to eat, but most of the day was spent getting the necessities set up.

Throughout the day, more lost travelers found their way to the castle. I estimate we're housing close to fifty of them now, and I already know Dreyden won't be happy about it when he returns from Tartarus. But what am I supposed to do about it?

Helping these people get settled in and providing for their basic needs while they have nothing feels *right*.

I feel a little bit more like myself for the first time in a very, very long time. My head feels clear and after my meltdown this morning, I feel a little less emotion. I'm not as on edge as yesterday, and I think it's because these people are filling my cup.

Funny and sweet, the lost fae travelers make me smile while filling my heart with the best feeling. All day long they came to me, seeking guidance and instruction once they'd finished a task.

Dreyden said they're creepy and look at me weird, but I think they're looking for a friend. Someone to lean on while they're trapped in this state of confusion.

It's clear this isn't a case of falling and hitting one's head. This is far beyond that, and there's more at play here. The healers check over each lost traveler as they arrive but can't find anything physically wrong with them, and they aren't sensing a spell cast over them.

My suspicion is that it's a powerful spell, more powerful than anything the healers have seen. But why? Why would someone wipe the memories of so many people? What could they have possibly done to get their memories taken from them?

Then it hits me.

Or what could they have seen?

I've been mulling it over, and I don't know how to get to the bottom of this. The travelers are arriving from all directions, not just one traceable location we could follow back to the source. Izan sent out several units from the legion, but they couldn't find any pattern produced by the lost travelers. It's like they're dropping out of thin air and then wandering toward the castle. I don't know what to make of it, but I'm determined to get to the bottom of it. These people need answers, and in my heart, I know I'm the one that'll find them.

Lyra decided to join me in dining outdoors with the lost travelers, and I couldn't be more grateful to have a friend like her.

She's kind, intuitive, and considerate. She's always there when I need her, and she knew I needed her this evening when Dreyden didn't show up for dinner.

Thea and Revna have their plates full right now with nearly fifty guests, but they're somehow managing to keep up. We've been served a buffet-style feast.

"Mmm," Lyra moans as she chews a mouth full of roasted chicken. "I don't know how they do it, but each meal Revna and Thea make is even better than the last."

All I've managed to eat today was the chocolate muffin Revna left for me after my breakdown. I watched the lost travelers eat earlier this afternoon, but I was so caught up in talking with these people I completely forgot to feed myself. My stomach hadn't growled until now as I watch Lyra stake bites of chicken with her fork and then slide them through thick brown gravy.

Unable to wait any longer, I pick up my utensils, cutting into a juicy slice of roast. Before bringing it to my mouth I scoop up a forkful of creamy mashed potatoes to go with it. It steams on the way to my mouth, filling my nose with the most savory scents. My eyes roll back slightly as I inhale deeper, making my mouth water and my stomach growl even louder.

I wrap my mouth around my fork, slowly sliding it out between my lips as I take in the bold flavors dancing across my tongue. "They always use the perfect amount of rosemary in the roast," I moan between bites.

Lyra and I sound like we're getting off to our plates full of food, and honestly, it doesn't feel that far off. Fire Court food is like nothing I've ever tasted, and it only continues to get better as the months go on.

Someone slides a plate containing two slices of cheesecake between me and Lyra, prompting us to look up at the same time.

Arryn stands across the table from us, grinning from ear to ear. "You both mentioned your love for cheesecake earlier. They just brought it out and I knew I had to snag you each a slice."

My heart skips a beat, and I hear Lyra suck in a gasp as her heart does the same.

Formal as always, Lyra praises Arryn for his gift, "That was thoughtful Arryn. Thank you for remembering."

I nod in agreement. "You worked your ass off today, and now you're spoiling us with cheesecake. What did we do to deserve this?"

His eyes light up, revealing how much he loves the acknowledgment "What did you do?" he raises a brow at me. "You've done *everything* for me. Not only for me but for everyone here."

Several people eating behind Arryn hear our conversation and join him in thanking me.

"You've saved us," one woman says.

"We don't know what we would have done without you," the man beside her says.

They begin applauding, joining in one at a time until there are nearly fifty people surrounding me, clapping together as they shout my name in praise.

"Lady Adeena!" they yell, sending chills down my spine.

No one has ever called me "lady" other than Dreyden. The words leaving their lips spark excitement, and it feels like something has snapped into place, but I can't quite put my finger on it.

These people need help, and I'm there for them. Now, they're looking at me like I'm their leader, and I can't say I hate it.

I'm kind of loving it.

THUNDER CRASHES outside my cathedral windows, jolting me awake as it shakes the entire castle. Lightning flashes, assaulting the night as it lights the land. The water glass on the stand next to my bed vibrates as the thunder rolls through.

My heart pounds as I gather my senses, glancing around the room as the electric currents illuminate the room around me.

There's no one there, but dread washes over me.

It's the middle of the night and the rain is coming down in thick sheets. It's impossible to see more than a few feet outside of the windows.

I feel for Dreyden next to me, but he's nowhere to be found. I pull the plush comforter back to be sure he's nowhere in this massive bed.

He hadn't shown up for dinner, but I assumed he was working off steam in Tartarus while he was hurt and mad at me, but what if it's more than that? What if something happened to him?

Panic strikes me, forcing my body to move.

"IZAN!" I scream as I jump out of bed, grabbing my robe on the way out. I run down the hall as fast as I can in search of the second-in-command.

"IZAN!" I repeat, calling for him as I turn down the hallway to his bed chambers. He's probably sleeping at this hour, but I don't care.

Dreyden is missing. My mate is missing.

If something happened to him after we exchanged such hurtful words this morning I'll never forgive myself.

I raise my fist to slam it into Izan's door, but it swings open just as my hand strikes. Izan jumps back, nearly missing my hit.

"What's wrong?" he asks, matching my panicked state.

"Dreyden didn't come back." I'm out of breath and struggling to get the words out.

"I noticed he wasn't back for dinner, but I assumed he would be back by nightfall. You're sure he's not here?" His voice calms slightly, but I think he's still worried. He's trying to be calm for me.

I can't stay calm in a time like this.

"I-I don't know. He always comes to bed and it's the middle of the night. Where else would he be?"

"I'll check his office," says a familiar voice from behind Izan.

I peek around Izan, finding Lyra curled up in a chair... in Izan's bed chambers. She rises to her feet, immediately coming to my side.

Izan grabs a tunic off the back of a chair next to Lyra as he heads for the door. "And I'll check the kitchen. If he's not there I'll alert the legion."

"I'll go with you," I say to Lyra as Izan shuts his door.

We hurry down the hall, nearly sprinting as fast as I ran to find Izan. Lyra isn't as fast as I am, so I beat her there by a few seconds.

I grip the door knob, forcing the door open in the blink of an eye. I take a step inside, realizing the room is quiet and still. It's dark and based on the stagnant smell, he hasn't been in here for days.

"He's not here," I whisper through broken breaths.

Lyra comes to a halt behind me as she finally reaches the door to his office. "Go get dressed, then we'll find him." Her voice is grim, and I know she's worried.

Dreyden *always* comes to bed. There hasn't been a single night he didn't, even after our biggest fights. He always comes back to me.

"I'll be fine in this," I accidentally snap at my friend before giving her an apologetic look.

"No, you won't," she says, eying my silky robe that does very little to conceal my naked body underneath.

I roll my eyes, knowing she's right but not wanting to waste time. "I'll meet you at the front entrance in five minutes."

"I'll find Izan then we'll be there."

"Okay," I nod as I choke back rising tears.

She sees the pain in my eyes, and she instinctively grabs hold of my hand, drawing it toward her chest as she cups it between her hands. "It's going to be okay, Adeena. I'm sure he's fine." She pulls me into a hug, not giving me the option to resist. "It's going to be okay," she repeats as she holds the back of my head with one hand, forcing me into a tighter hug.

I hug her back as silent tears begin rolling down my face. "I was annoyed with him this morning and I said some things I regret. I told him he was not needed here... and I know that's not true. I *do* need him, but I can't have him constantly breathing down my throat like he has been since I almost died. It's not fair."

She pulls back to stare into my eyes. Her jade-green eyes draw me in with one look. "You can tell him that when he gets back."

Gods, I hope she's right.

Dreyden and I need to work on our communication, and that starts the second he gets back here.

"Go get dressed," she gently reminds me. "See you in five."

I don't hesitate as I turn away from her, running back down the maze of halls back to my bed chambers. The marble feels cold with each barefoot step I take, and my feet slap against the floor, echoing down the hallway. It's a sound that'll haunt me forever if Dreyden isn't okay.

WE'VE BEEN SEARCHING for Dreyden for hours with zero luck. There's no sign of him ever returning from Tartarus. He never sent word to tell us he wasn't coming back tonight, and that's what scares me most.

The legion has been out in the rain all night, searching every inch of Fire Court they can. Everyone is sopping wet and exhausted, worried sick for their high lord.

I'm a ball of tears, barely holding myself together. I've had to step in and out of the bathing chambers several times for a few minutes of alone time. I bawl my eyes out, hyperventilating into a towel so no one hears me, and then I return to the front entrance to wait beside Izan. He doesn't say anything when he sees my red eyes and puffy cheeks, he only gives me a sympathetic smile before reluctantly giving me the same update over and over again: no sign of Dreyden.

Arryn and the lost travelers joined in on the search when they caught wind of my missing mate. He keeps checking on me to make sure I'm all right. Izan seems annoyed with his presence in the castle while Dreyden is missing, but it's nice to have someone checking in on me.

"The darkest night end will end in the most beautiful dawn. You will get your sunrise, Lady Adeena," Arryn says each time he stops by the main entrance. His silver eyes are kind, and I see so much potential in him as a lifelong friend.

"Why is this guy so artsy with his words?" Izan whispers when Arryn finally leaves for the night.

I let out a light, forced laugh. "I think you're jealous. He's witty and sharp with his tongue. You may know your way around a sword, but he could probably cripple an opponent with one sentence."

That's perhaps an exaggeration, but it's a hilarious thought.

Izan scoffs, rolling his eyes as his lips twitch upward. He's hiding a smile.

Lyra went to bed hours ago, along with most other people inside the castle.

"You need to get some rest," Izan says beside me as the sunrise begins peeking through the windows.

We've been pacing near the front entrance all night. Izan has stayed cool, calm, and collected throughout the entirety of the night, and I, on the other hand, continue to have breakdowns.

"I can rest when Dreyden is found," I sigh through a yawn, rays of stray sunlight burning my eyes as the sun climbs over the horizon. This is only the hundredth time he has told me to go to bed.

"If he returns while you're sleeping, I'll have someone get you right away." He's no longer asking me to go to bed, but he's *telling* me to.

I stand there, mulling over my answer in silence for a few minutes while he stares at me with his hands folded behind his back. He looks surprisingly energetic, but he isn't the one who's been crying over their mate all night long.

"Fine," I eventually concede as I raise my fist at him in a threatening manner. "You better wake me up if he comes back."

He raises his hands in defense. "I will, Adeena. Go to bed."

"Thank you. Goodnight," I say as I leave the main entrance, padding down the hallways back toward my bed chambers.

Once inside our room, I slip out of the clothes I've been wearing all night long and into my favorite lace and silk robe. Into *Dreyden's* favorite robe.

Climbing into our massive, empty bed, I allow sleep to consume me quickly. My eyes are too heavy to fight my exhaustion, and my body is physically drained from pacing all night. My power reserves feel depleted from the amount of energy I've used throughout the night. My body pulled from my power reserves to self-sustain, but it only goes so far.

I fall into a deep sleep, picturing my mate as my mind fades.

Chapter Nine

DREYDEN

My power depletion hangover is better than I expected it to be this morning. I originally planned on portaling back to Fire Court as soon as I woke, but an overenthusiastic Alaric was already up, packing our supply-drop bags.

"I tried to convince him to stay, but he won't listen." Ellia wipes her hands on her apron, dusting excess flour from her hands as she side-eyes Alaric. She's whipping up cinnamon rolls this morning with the cinnamon she pulled from my bag yesterday, and they smell fucking incredible. My stomach growls at the smell of the dough alone, I can't even imagine how they'll smell while they're baking.

"He's a man on a mission, Ellia," I say as I shovel fork-fulls of scrambled eggs into my mouth. "I'll take care of him. I promise."

Her eyes rise as she looks up from the sticky dough in her hands, burning a hole through me as she glares. "If he gets too weak, you need to force him to come back. You're in deep shit if you don't."

"We'll be fine," Alaric says as he walks into the kitchen. He scoops a slice of toast off the counter as he throws a bag over his back. "Let's go."

I nod, scarfing down the final bites of scrambled eggs as fast as I can. "We should be done early today. An early start means an early finish. I'll head back to Fire Court as soon as we finish."

"Your mate is probably worried sick," Ellia sighs as she begins rolling out the cinnamon dough.

"I'm sure she's fine," I bite out more angrily than intended as I rip into a piece of buttery toast. "This is more important right now."

She lets out a long sigh, pressing her judgment into the dough. "If you say so."

Alaric gives Ellia a warm embrace and a soft kiss on the forehead. It's the same loving routine every morning, and I'll never get sick of witnessing such tender love.

He leads the way out, and I follow closely behind with our cart of supplies. We didn't have our usual supplies from Fire Court because I stayed here last night, but Alaric has plenty of extra in the storage room below his house. We began pulling supplies from there as soon as we woke.

"We've got three drop-off points this morning. The fourth one has too many looters in the area, so we won't risk tipping them off."

How Alaric already knows this information, I don't know, but I don't question him. He has eyes and ears all over this village and far beyond. He's the eyes and ears of the underground supply chain.

Nearly an hour after departing Alaric's family home, we arrive at the first drop-off point. It normally takes us less time, but looters are out in higher-than-normal numbers today, and we're doing our best to remain undetected. Even though I can easily take them out, we can't draw attention to ourselves. It would be no different from ringing a dinner bell, calling out to everyone in the area, letting them know we've arrived with a cart full of food. Not only would we be swarmed by looters, but starving people as well. It would be too hard to tell who's who amid the chaos, and we'd risk hurting innocent people.

We descend a short flight of moss-covered rock stairs leading toward a notoriously creaky wooden door. This supply drop is hidden in the basement beneath an abandoned bar. The liquor was wiped clean soon after the war ended. It now fuels looters with enough drunken rage and anger to do what they do best, steal and destroy.

Too many good people turned bad after the war. They lost themselves in a fight for their lives, choosing evil over good to make it out on top. I wish I could say I wouldn't do the same if I were in a similar situation, but I don't know... I think I'd do what I must, especially for Adeena.

Then again, Adeena doesn't want my help.

Taking one last look around, my voice is barely a whisper as I glance at Alaric behind me. "You know what to do if you see someone."

He nods as he steadies his breathing. His body is weak and less healed than what would be ideal for a venture into town, but his determination to feed the people of Tartarus can't be stopped. Giving me a quick nod, he turns his back, facing toward the street to keep watch.

We keep things consistent at each drop-off, which leaves less room for error when every day is this dangerous. Alaric keeps watch while I clear the interior location. If he detects anyone he whistles, alerting me to possible danger. Sometimes it's merely a traveler passing through, and others it's an actual threat, such as a band of looters or feral creatures. After I'm done clearing each location I send out a butterfly spy, signaling it's safe for him to join me inside. We quickly make the drop, then slip out the door faster than we came. When we aren't busy making drop-offs, Alaric networks the underground community across

Tartarus, spreading word of the hidden supplies to the right people.

The wooden door creaks as I open it, making us both cringe. I leave the door open behind me as I slip inside. It's dark and reeks of mold, just the way we like it. Uninviting is better for keeping unwanted strays away. It appears to be abandoned, like nearly every other building in this ghost town, making it a discrete location to hide supplies.

Dusty bookshelves draped in cobwebs make this room a little ominous, even for me. The deep shelves offer an abundance of places to hide as I creep my way down the dimly lit rows.

I reach out with my senses, feeling around as I walk, searching for any hint of magic hiding within the space. The air is stagnant and I don't feel anything unusual, so I keep going.

Five minutes pass and I've cleared the entire space. Swirling my fingertips over my palm, I create a tiny golden butterfly to send back to Alaric. Gold dust follows the butterfly as it leaps from my hand, launching itself into the air. It soars out of sight as I make my way toward the back of the room where we keep the supplies hidden behind a wall of empty crates. We strategically draped old tarps around the clever arrangement of crates. At first glance, the wall of crates appears to be the end of the room, but if you know where you're going, there's a tunnel leading to the small stock of supplies.

The tunnel is so small I nearly have to crawl, but if I fold in my wings and crouch low enough, I'm able to make it through.

Alaric fits through the tunnel more easily than I can, but it's still a bit of a squeeze.

I slowly make my way through the tunnel, avoiding newly spun cobwebs as I go. The spiders do a phenomenal job of keeping up the "abandoned" look and feel of this place. No one in their right mind would wander through this tunnel unless they knew what lies on the other side.

My jaw drops and my stomach sinks as I step out of the tunnel.

It's empty.

Totally, completely, utterly empty.

Six days a week isn't enough for these starving people. We carry as much as we possibly can without drawing attention to ourselves, but it just isn't enough. The demand for food is growing far beyond what the two of us are capable of supplying.

"Fuck," Alaric curses under his breath as he steps out from the tunnel behind me. He's shaking his head in disbelief as he speaks the words I was already thinking. "We need more help."

I pull the cart of supplies to the middle of the space and then pull out a bag full of dried beans. "Yeah, but who? No one wants to risk their lives for this place."

Alaric begins unloading bags of rice on the opposite side of the small space. "That's because they don't understand."

Sadness takes me by surprise as I reminisce, knowing exactly who he's referring to. The brief meetings with the other Archai courts and my shaken friendship with Hali are still fresh in my mind. "I tried, Alaric, but they didn't care. No one wants to risk depleting their supplies until Tartarus can be self-sufficient again, and the only way to do that is to rid Tartarus of criminals and loose creatures."

"Why don't they send in help? Surely the courts could get the prison up and running again."

We've been over this a hundred times, and it's the same conversation over and over again. Alaric believes my high title comes with a high reward, but that's not always true. I can't dictate what the other courts do and I can't drain my own court dry to help a fallen kingdom on the other side of the continent. I bring what I can from Fire Court, but we both know it's not enough. I can aid the people, but I can't supply an entire kingdom on my own.

"At a cost," I sigh. "These things all cost the courts both monetarily and materially, and there's no reward. The Wychwood Forest shields them from the chaos ensuing over here. It allows them to turn a blind eye to what's really going on. It's not fair, but I don't know what else to do."

"That's the game, isn't it?" Alaric's voice is more somber than normal. "These kingdoms play the ranks, stabbing each other in the back when it's convenient, only offering aid when there's a reward working in their favor. There's no room for charity work in the game of politics."

He isn't wrong, and that's what pains me the most.

As High Lord, it's my duty to protect my people at all costs, and Tartarus does not fall under that blanket. I can't take supplies from my people, depriving them of what they've always had and known. I've taken what won't be missed, but if I take more it'll impact *my* people. The very people I swore an oath to protect and serve.

If I deprive them to help a kingdom most of my people have never been to, what will they think of me? What will be the consequence of putting another kingdom above my own?

The answer is clear. I'd be overthrown by my own people, kicked aside, and forced to leave. They'd send me running back to Tartarus, and Tartarus would be worse off than if I'd just continued doing what I'm doing now. My weekly supply drops would cease, and there would be zero assistance from Fire Court. Famine would take the people, and few would survive. There would be no coming back from it.

I must be smart. There are risks and rewards with everything I do, and regardless I must maintain the balance. Fire Court has put their trust in me, and I can't let them down.

I turn to Alaric, offering him a pathetic smile to lighten the mood. "We'll figure it out."

"We're running out of time," Alaric scoffs as we finish unloading the supplies.

He has never said it directly, but I know he holds judgment against me for not doing more. I wish I could do more, but I haven't figured out a way yet.

We finish our supply drops by mid-morning. Each drop-off location was completely empty, so Alaric and I have decided we'll do a second drop-off this afternoon. The plan is for Alaric to rest up while I portal back to Fire Court for more supplies. It should only take me a couple of hours to check in on Adeena and gather supplies.

Standing in Alaric's kitchen, I dig into a warm cinnamon roll. My eyes flutter to the back of my head as I sink my teeth into it. "I'll meet you back here as soon as I'm done filling the portal with supplies. Rest up while I'm gone."

"Oh, he will. Neither of you should be going anyway," Ellia scolds. "Your power reserves are still too low," she says to me before turning her anger toward Alaric. "And you, sir, need to rest. You're not fully healed and you're doing your body a disservice by abusing it like this."

She was enraged as soon as Alaric mentioned we would be going back out this afternoon. I understand why she's upset, but after seeing the empty shelves inside each supply drop, we knew we needed to be doing more. We finished earlier than normal, which left plenty of time to do one more drop this afternoon. We're doing what we must.

Alaric rolls his eyes from across the kitchen. "I'll be fine."

Ellia says nothing as she glares at him. She's being protective of her lover, and I can't blame her for trying to stop him.

"See you in a few hours. Thank you again, Ellia," I say as I hold up what's left of my cinnamon roll.

Once outside, I open a portal back to the front lawn of Fire Court.

I exhale loudly, trying my best to release the tension I've been holding over Adeena. Shaking my hands at my sides, I let go of our fight as I step inside.

We need a fresh start today.

Chapter Ten

ADEENA

W hite light filters through the slits of my eyelids. It stings my sensitive, tired eyes, and I clamp them shut, rolling myself deeper into the plush feather comforter. Its warmth wraps around me, pulling me back toward a deep sleep I desperately need.

Loud voices outside my door force my eyes back open, and reality sets in. I gasp for air as I sit up.

My eyes immediately land on the cathedral windows lining the walls of my bed chambers. I'd meant to sleep for an hour or two, but by the look of the sun, I've slept through the morning and high noon is quickly approaching.

"Fuck," I curse as I swing my legs over the side of my bed, then race toward the doors.

My hands land on the handles of the double doors, and I pull them open with all my strength. They swing so hard that they slam into the wall on both sides, and I hear the wall crack under the pressure. I'm still not used to the super-human strength that came with becoming fae.

I'm immediately blocked by Izan's broad body, his hand raised like he was about to knock on my door.

"Where is he?" I ask, frantically peering around Izan's shoulders in search of my mate.

He lowers his hand, settling it at his side as he opens his mouth, "He's-"

I can't wait any longer. The words aren't spilling from his mouth fast enough. I have to get to Dreyden.

I push past him, catching him by surprise as I force him out of my way. He steps aside but reaches for my arm. I avoid his grip as I begin running down the hallway.

"Adeena!" Izan shouts from behind me, but I keep running. "Adeena!" he repeats louder this time.

"Why did you let me sleep so long?" I yell as I continue my panicked search for Dreyden.

I glance into each open door as I pass, searching for a glimpse of him. If he's hurt I'll never forgive myself for the way I spoke to him yesterday. My words were hurtful and he deserves better from me.

Izan's boots collide with the marble floors as he starts after me. He's shouting after me, but his words are a blur as the seconds pass by. My heart pounds in my chest harder than I've ever felt before, and I swear it's going to bruise.

Closing in on the front entrance, I hear Izan gaining ground behind me.

"Adeena, wait!" His voice echoes against the giant doors as I force them open. "You can't go out there!"

He's too late.

Sunlight floods my eyes, blinding me momentarily while my pupils adjust to the outside world. I take a step into the light, shielding my eyes as I cautiously walk onto the landing overlooking the steps down to the front lawn.

My jaw falls as my eyes focus beyond the castle steps.

An audience of fae at least ten thousand strong crowd the lawn, and they're all watching *me*.

"Wha…" The words are caught in my throat, choking air from my lungs. "What is this?" I ask Izan, feeling his powerful presence behind me.

"Adeena, you need to get back inside," Izan's voice is a warning behind me, but I don't understand.

Why would Izan stop me from seeing this? Why are these people here?

And why are they so focused on me?

"Adeena," Izan growls behind me, sending a shiver down my back. He never talks to me like this.

Throwing my hands up, I twist to meet his glare. As I turn, I feel the breeze slip by my bare stomach, opening the scandalous robe I'd slipped into this morning before crawling into bed.

Izan's eyes widen at the unfiltered view of my naked body. "I tried to tell you."

I snatch the robe in my hands, clenching it shut, but the entire thing is made of thin silk and lace. Closing it does little to hide my bare body. My cheeks warm as humiliation washes over me.

If I'd stopped to listen to Izan's warning and not run out here like a crazed lunatic lost without her mate, I would have saved myself from a world of embarrassment.

"Wrap her in this," Revna orders Izan as she holds a woven blanket through the entryway.

Izan doesn't hesitate to take it from her, quickly unfolding the white material as he crosses the landing. "Here," he says as he holds it up, gesturing for me to step into it.

"Thank you," I whisper as Izan drapes the blanket around me, covering my far too exposed body.

Lyra appears in the entryway behind us, gasping the words as she steps outside with us, "Oh my. What is going on?"

Izan shakes his head as he crosses his arms over his rock-hard chest. "I don't know. They arrived a few minutes ago and they're asking for Adeena."

I eye Izan as I ask, "They're asking for me? Why?"

"They won't say. They just keep asking for you and they won't talk to anyone."

Lyra rests her hand over my shoulder in the most comforting way as she comes to my side.. "That explains why they're all staring at you."

Scanning the crowd, I search for any possible familiar faces, but there are so many that they're impossible to focus on.

People in the crowd begin talking, taking some of the pressure off me as their volume increases. They're all still staring at me, but less alarmed now that I've been given a blanket.

I watch the people for a moment, unsure what to do from here.

A tall, lengthy woman toward the front of the group pushes her way forward, emerging at the bottom of the stairs. She takes a step forward, but she's quickly stopped by a strong wall of legion guards.

"Let her through," I call out before I know what I'm saying.

I don't know why I said it, but I did. Something about her is drawing me in, compelling me to speak with her.

A guard turns around to make eye contact with Izan, waiting for him to grant my request.

He hesitates, but after a stern look from me, he nods toward the guard, repeating my words, "Let her through."

"Thank you," I whisper.

He leans toward me, speaking so quietly only the two of us can hear, "You better be onto something here."

I clear my throat and clasp my hands, waiting for the woman to clear the stairs. She has silver eyes similar to my own, and her dirty blonde hair falls to her shoulders, swaying as she ascends the stairs.

As I take in the sight of the unfamiliar woman, I catch a glimpse of what I think is a familiar face, and I lean to see around him, but her large frame blocks most of my view. I take a step to the side as my heart begins to pound, quickening with each passing second.

The woman reaches the top of the stairs just as *he* comes into focus.

Dreyden.

Sudden relief washes over me, and I let out the breath I'd been holding. I feel like I'm breathing for the first time since last night.

He's staring at me, just like everyone else around me, and he appears to be somewhere between pissed off and concerned, but

I don't care. I don't care about the fight we got into yesterday, and I don't care about his over-protective, possessive attitude.

Seeing him makes the tension and anger melt away, and in this moment all I need is to be with him, tangled in his arms while he sweeps me off my feet into the tightest embrace.

Stepping around the woman, I begin to descend the stairs, forgetting we're surrounded by thousands of strangers. Time seems to stand still, and I can't get to him fast enough.

I'm halfway down the stairs when I'm suddenly pulled from my hypnotic trance.

"Are you... Adeena Devna?"

I freeze on the stairs, hesitantly withdrawing my eyes from Dreyden. I turn to meet the eyes of the unfamiliar woman at the top of the castle steps. "What?" I question, confused as to how she knows my name.

Her eyes are locked on mine as she repeats his words, "Are you Adeena Devna, High Lady of Sky?"

Chapter Eleven

DREYDEN

My world stands still as the words leave her mouth.

"Are you Adeena Devna, High Lady of Sky?" the unfamiliar face asks my mate.

How the fuck does she know her name? And why does she call her by the name bestowed upon her by the gods?

Adeena's lips part as her jaw drops slightly. Her chest rises as she inhales a sharp, sudden breath. Her eyes leave the unidentified woman to find me, and I know she needs me.

The crowd breaks out in a frenzied panic, screaming and yelling for Adeena. She's overwhelmed by the deafening chaos, looking between me and the thousands of fae standing on my front lawn. There's a flood of emotion flowing through her devastatingly beautiful face.

I can't push my way through the crowd quickly enough, so I unfold my wings, shoving a few people backward in the process. My wings beat hard as I bend my knees, then jump, catching hold of the air with my wings. I rise over the massive crowd, clearing the tops of their heads as I fly toward my mate. Most of the fae are so distracted by Adeena that they don't even bat an eye at my powerful presence.

I hit the ground next to Adeena with a thunderous force, and her arms are already outstretched, waiting for me. I snake one arm around the small of her back, pulling her against me while I use my other hand to cup the back of her head as I kiss her. She's shaking at first, but she quickly stills, melting against me as I tighten my grip around her.

Her bottom lip is the last thing to stop trembling as I suck it into my mouth. Her hands rest against my chest, gripping my shirt as she kisses me back.

"I missed you," she breathes against my lips as our kiss comes to an end, interrupted by the uproar around us.

"I missed you, too," I smile before planting a soft kiss on her forehead.

"What's going on here?" I ask as I turn away from her, facing the unidentified woman. "And who are you?"

She opens her mouth to speak, but the voices filling the air around us are too much. They're becoming so loud I can hardly hear myself think. She closes her mouth, looking around as the shouting increases.

Izan stands behind Adeena, throwing his hands up in frustration. He gestures toward his ears, signaling to me that he can't hear himself think either.

My patience has worn thin by the lack of respect, so I clear my throat, preparing my voice as I stalk toward the edge of the landing overlooking the front lawn. "SILENCE!" I roar, my voice ripping through the crowd.

But, it has no effect. Absolutely none, zero.

I clear my throat once more. "SILENCE," I repeat louder this time.

Still, nothing. They're not paying the slightest attention to me. Their eyes are focused on Adeena, and they're yelling for her.

Flames light at my fingertips as my anger is fueled by their blatant disrespect for the high lord of the court they're currently standing in. How dare they show up here uninvited, demand my mate's undivided attention, then ignore my commands.

As I'm about to explode, I feel a gentle hand on my arm. I look down to find Adeena at my side, eyeing me with those stunning sterling eyes.

"Let me try," she mouths over the crowd.

I nod, taking a step back for my mate, but I don't think it'll work. If they can't be bothered by my booming voice, it's going to take a lot more show of force to catch their attention.

But I must let her try. If I don't, she'll be even more mad at me than she was yesterday.

She takes another step forward, and now she's standing at the very edge of the landing overlooking the lawn. She stands there in silence for a moment, straightening her back and correcting her posture as she eyes the crowd.

They're watching her, and they quickly catch on. One by one they shut their mouths, and silence falls upon the lawn.

I'm fairly certain my jaw hits the ground while I watch her. She hasn't said a word, yet this crowd ten thousand strong gives her their unwavering attention, quietly waiting for her to speak.

She watches them for a moment, wrapped in the blanket Revna brought for her after she ran outside in nothing but that stupid fucking lace robe I love so much.

That robe should have been for my eyes only, and now not only has this entire group of people have seen her in it, but so have my castle staff, legion soldiers, and my second-in-command. It infuriates me to no end as to why she was beyond the doors of our bed chambers in such attire, and I'll have this chat with her later when there aren't ten thousand people standing on my front lawn.

Once she has their undivided attention, she turns to face the unfamiliar woman still standing on the landing with us. "Why are you asking for me?"

The woman is nervous now that all eyes are on her and Adeena. Her voice cracks as she says, "Zeus spoke to me in a dream."

Adeena takes a step closer to her. "And what did Zeus tell you in this dream?" Her voice is far more calm than mine would be.

"He told me to find High Lady of Sky, Adeena Devna. He showed me visions of you, then he kept repeating 'defender of the forgotten...'"

Adeena suddenly holds her hand up, cutting off the woman's word. She gravitates her attention back to the crowd as she rotates her body toward them.

Her voice is clear, calm, and commanding as she speaks. "The Fire Court soldiers will escort you to the legion camp we've set up. You will wait for further instructions once you are there. All your questions will be answered soon enough."

"I'll get the rest of the legion out here to assist," Izan says as thousands of people begin to move, following Adeena's command without hesitation.

The woman on the landing starts for the stairs, falling in line with the rest of the people exiting the lawn.

"Wait," Adeena calls to her. "I'd like you to come inside with us."

The woman turns on her heel and then walks back up the stairs, following Adeena through the castle doors.

Izan remains by my side, waiting for my approval of Adeena's plan before assembling the legion. "Are you okay with this?" he asks as soon as she's far enough away she won't hear us.

Running my hands through my hair I sigh, "Yes. I don't have an alternative plan and we need to figure out what's going on. Do you have any other ideas?"

A frown turns his lips upside down. "No," he shrugs. "I don't have a plan that won't royally piss off Adeena."

I don't either. My instinctual reaction is to send all these people away, back to wherever they came from, but I know Adeena won't let that happen without a fight. Additionally, I need to know why these people are here and who sent them. There's more at play than this many lost fae showing up at my castle doors.

I don't know who's behind this, but I'm going to find out.

"Get the legion out here and get these people set up. I saw some children amongst the crowd and we need to make sure they're fed. I'll be inside with Adeena and that woman. I'm sure Adeena is already questioning her."

Izan nods, "I'll keep you updated throughout the day."

"Thank you," I say as I walk back inside the castle, leaving Izan to babysit at least ten thousand people.

Knowing Adeena, she *very* likely took that woman to the dining hall for some food. She can't let guests go hungry, and I'm sure that's the first thing she asked the woman when they entered the castle.

I follow the long hallways down to the dining hall, listening to the clack of my boots echo off the marble floors as I walk. It's eerily quiet here compared to the chaos ensuing in Tartarus, and sometimes it sends chills down my spine knowing how good we have it here. It's not fair to the people of Tartarus.

Adeena's soft voice drifts down the hall, warming my insides as I get closer. A smile reaches my lips as I listen to her laugh and talk. She's easy to talk to and she gets along with just about anyone. The conversations she can strike up with a complete stranger blow my mind, and it's not a talent I possess. Although, I can't say I put much effort into talking with people I don't know.

I round the corner to the dining hall, and my eyes immediately fall upon my mate seated at the dining table, casually munching on some green grapes as the woman beside her eats leftover roasted chicken.

Adeena's eyes meet mine and a radiant smile lights her face. She waves me over, gesturing to the seat across from her. "Come in. We were chatting and getting something to eat while we waited for you."

I raise an eyebrow, unsure why she would have waited for me when this was going to go her way regardless. Crossing the room, I try to be friendly as I ask, "What is your name?"

The dirty blonde, silver-eyed woman raises her eyes from her plate as I take a seat across from her and Adeena. "Edlynne, sir," she says as she lowers her head, respectfully bowing.

At least she has manners. That's more than I can say for the rest of the fae outside.

Adeena leans forward in her chair, focusing on me. "Edlynne was telling me she doesn't know how she got here, or why there are so many others outside."

"So what *do* you remember then? You mentioned Zeus coming to you in a dream. What happened in the dream and what did you do after the dream to end up here?"

Edlynne sets her fork on her plate gently and then places her hands in her lap. She looks between the two of us as she begins telling her story. "Zeus visited me in a dream. He told me we've been locked away for our safety, and we're free now that Adeena Devna has been named High Lady of Sky."

"Did he say anything else in this dream?" I ask, doing my best to hide the skepticism in my voice.

"He said we need to find the high lady, Adeena Devna now that we've been released under her protection. He kept repeating 'defender of the forgotten.'"

Adeena shifts in her chair, her face suddenly changing to a much more serious expression.

Chapter Twelve

Defender of the forgotten, keeper of divine ability, yielder to none.

The words play on repeat as a deep male voice echoes through my head.

My mouth is dry, and I feel a shift in my power. It's like my power reserves are recharging but on a much more exponential level. A sweat breaks out across my forehead as his voice continues.

Defender of the forgotten, keeper of divine ability, yielder to none.

Chills wash over me as sweat begins to roll down my back. I'm having trouble staying focused on the conversation. The second the words left Edlynne's mouth 'defender of the forgotten' I felt the change, a sudden click somewhere deep within me.

Defender of the forgotten, keeper of divine ability, yielder to none.

"Protected from what?" Dreyden asks Edlynne, and the voice in my head comes to a stop.

I look up, watching Dreyden and Edlynne, wondering if they'd just experienced the same thing I did, or if they're about to think I'm crazy when I tell them what just occurred in my mind. Edlynne already sounds like she's lost her mind, so maybe she won't bat an eye, but Dreyden will be ready to take me down to the healer's clinic.

Shaking her head side to side, Edlynne says, "I don't know. It's like my memories have been wiped clean. I feel like I know so much, but when I search for the information there's nothing there. It's empty."

"Do you remember anything before the dream?" I ask.

Her face drops as her visible frustration grows. "No," she sighs. "I was dreaming of Zeus, then he left the dream and I woke up on the forest floor, surrounded by crimson red foliage and fireflies. It was dark, but the fireflies led me here. I followed them through the forest and by the time the sun rose I could see the castle in the distance. I ran into all these other people in the forest on my way here. None of us know what's going on, and to tell you the truth, we're all frightened." Tears well in her bottom eyelids. "Who would do this to us?"

I take her hand, clenching it tightly for reassurance. "I don't know, but we're going to figure it out. Until then, you'll stay in the legion camp just outside the castle. We'll take care of you."

Edlynne's face relaxes just enough to clear the tears from her eyes. "How can I help?"

Rising to my feet, I look at Dreyden across the table. He's quietly watching us, mulling over the answers Edlynne provided us with. He looks skeptical, but he isn't saying anything. My eyes return to Edlynne. "You'll be of use in the legion camp. I'm sure they need help getting more tents set up. There will be quite a few of you in each tent, and I'm hoping we have enough. If not, we'll figure it out."

One of the castle staff waits by the dining hall entrance, patiently waiting to take Edlynne back outside with the rest of the lost fae. I make eye contact with him, nodding as he understands what I need without saying anything. He crosses the room and then approaches Edlynne.

"I can show you where you'll be staying," he says with the politest tone, offering her his arm as she stands from her chair.

"That would be lovely. Thank you," she smiles, looping her arm through his.

"Edlynne," I call as they're about to exit the room. "I'll find you later this afternoon, but if you need me please ask one of our staff members to find me and they'll get me right away."

"Thank you, High Lady," she says as she bows her head toward me.

Chills run down my spine once more. I shiver slightly, feeling an overwhelming amount of power flowing through me.

I turn back to Dreyden once they've left, and he's watching me intently from his chair.

"What?" I ask, cocking my head to the side.

Dreyden stands and then circles around the table to stand at my side. He grabs my hands, pulling them around his waist as he steps closer. I hug him tightly, inhaling his intoxicating scent. Strong arms wrap around me as I breathe, melting against his hard body.

He's being gentle with me, more tender than normal, and his embrace is sweet and loving as he holds me.

"I love seeing you so in charge," he whispers into my ear. "But I hate whatever is going on here. She sounds truthful, but how do we know? I hate the way they were all screaming for you."

I step back, feeling the instant mix of emotions as he speaks the truth I don't want to hear. "They may have been overwhelmingly loud, but they weren't being the slightest bit aggressive."

He bites his bottom lip as he goes deep in thought. "No, they weren't being aggressive," he reluctantly agrees. "We need to get Izan in here to talk about what we're going to do with all these people."

"And Lyra too," I eye him.

Izan may be his second-in-command, but Lyra is mine in my mind. She's my best friend and she needs to be here for this conversation, especially if I'm going to stand any chance against Dreyden and Izan.

Dreyden rolls his eyes playfully. He already knew I'd need Lyra here.

A TINY BLACK butterfly leaves through an open window as Dreyden takes his seat at the conference table in his office.

He formed the butterfly before starting our meeting with Izan and Lyra to send Alaric a message in Tartarus. He was apparently planning on making a second trip back to Tartarus to do a supply drop with Alaric, but his plans have changed now that we have thousands of lost fae on the Fire Court lawn.

Between my chat with Edlynne and now, I managed to throw on a fresh set of clothes. I was ready to burn that scandalous robe to ash as I took it off, but I practiced deep breathing and taking control of my impulsive behavior, so I laid it on the bed for Dreyden to burn off my body later tonight after we talk about where the fuck he was last night.

Dreyden sits at the head of the table with me on his left and Izan on his right. Lyra sits to my right, dressed in her usual glamorous attire. Her thick black braids sit on top of her head today, twisted into an intricate woven design. Gold hoops loop through her ears, bringing even more glow to her face.

We've already updated Izan and Lyra on everything Edlynne told us, but we need to figure out where to go from here. What do we do with this many people? How long do we allow them to stay? Where will they go from here?

There are too many unknowns.

"How do we know that what she's saying is true?" Izan scoffs across from me. "How likely is it that Zeus himself appeared in her dream to deliver a message?"

"I don't think it's likely," Dreyden shakes his head. "But it's not impossible."

Lyra leans forward, joining in on the conversation. "The gods *chose* Adeena themselves to put an end to a prophecy that threatened to destroy us all. Don't you think it would be foolish to believe there isn't more going on here?"

"That was months ago," says Izan, eyeing Lyra.

Lyra's volume increases as she gets annoyed with Izan. "And? They titled her 'High Lady of Sky' and nothing has come of it. That title does not come without responsibility. Whether you'd like to admit it or not, it's the truth, and we need to be more open-minded than thinking there's ill-intent behind everything that happens."

Izan sits forward in his chair, using his knees to support his elbows as he says, "You want me to believe that the god of all gods visited this woman in a dream?"

"Yes," I snap, cutting him off.

Three sets of eyes land on me, taken aback by my abrupt end to their argument.

I swallow as the power pulsing through me rises to the surface of my skin, lighting my stars. Their eyes widen, and Lyra's jaw drops.

"There was a voice in my head when Edlynne said 'defender of the forgotten.' He kept repeating a mantra of some sort. His voice was deep and powerful, overwhelming, and electrifying. Something changed when Edlynne said those four words, and now I feel so much power running through me I can hardly think."

"You feel more power?" Dreyden asks as he watches my stars glow brighter.

I nod. "Yes. There's so much power I can feel my body vibrating, but somehow I feel more in control than ever. I don't know how to explain what I'm experiencing... There's a lot going on inside right now."

Izan's question comes next. "What was the mantra?"

"Defender of the forgotten, keeper of divine ability, yielder to none." As I say the words aloud my stars flash brighter, temporarily blinding everyone seated at the table. A jolt of energy pulses through me, making me jump out of my chair. I nearly fall backward, but Dreyden gets up and out of his chair before I can blink, catching me.

The light illuminating my stars begins to dim, leaving behind a metallic gloss around the outline of each star. They're molten, moving around my skin like they're doing a dance.

My power feels even more energized, even more significant than before. The battle for control I've been fighting for with myself feels like it has suddenly come to an end. There's a feeling of relief that sits in my chest, and I feel lighter even with all this energy buzzing through me.

"I told you," Lyra barks at Izan as they watch my stars. "The gods *are* involved here."

Izan glares at her, annoyed he was wrong.

"I agree," Dreyden nods with wide eyes. "What just happened?"

There's a strange look on his face, and it reminds me of how he looked at me the first few weeks after I turned fae. He couldn't keep his hands off me after my transition, and to be honest, I couldn't keep my hands off him either. We were like wild animals, constantly finding new places to have mind-blowing sex and sneakily touch each other like horny teenagers. Our busy schedules keep us more busy these days, but we find time for each other every day.

"My power reserve capacity increased earlier when Edlynne said the words, and it just now happened again when I said them." I feel the glistening metal branded into my skin. The texture of my skin is the same, but my stars have come to life, moving freely upon my skin.

"How is that possible?" Izan asks aloud, not to anyone in particular, mostly thinking out loud in disbelief.

Lyra shoots him another annoyed look. "Do you *really* need someone to explain this to you, or are you shocked you were proven wrong this quickly?"

He rolls his eyes, ignoring her sharp tongue.

I look between Lyra and Izan, watching the two of them banter back and forth as though they're an old married couple. They're picking at each other, but in some ways, it feels like friendly fire.

Dreyden releases his hold on me, allowing me to straighten as I look over my body.

"Are you okay?" he asks, his voice full of concern... and hunger? Maybe?

I inhale a sharp breath as he watches me with a predatory look. He steps closer, but I turn back toward the conference table to face Izan and Lyra, who have now stopped arguing and are watching us.

A low growl escapes Dreyden's throat as I slip from his grip.

It takes everything in me to not turn back to him, to plaster myself to his hard body and rip his clothes off.

But we have more pressing matters.

"Let's get down to business," I breathe. "What are we going to do with them?"

Dreyden's breath is hot on my neck as he stands behind me, sending waves of chills down my overly sensitive skin. "What choice do we have but to keep them here? If they are indeed linked to you, we can't send them away."

"True," Izan chimes in. "Do we have enough... food? For all these people? Supplies?"

I hadn't even thought of that. We don't have an exact number, but I was guessing there were well over ten thousand lost fae outside the castle this morning. Their numbers are overwhelming and I don't know what kind of back-up plan Dreyden has in place for things like this.

Then again, nothing like this has ever happened that I'm aware of. Ten thousand people don't just show up out of nowhere.

Until now.

I'm feeling every emotion possible, and I don't know what to make of it. I'm energized by the new power flowing through my body, but I'm unsure what to do or feel from here. The massive army of lost fae outside came here because they believed they were being led by Zeus. They're looking at me as their leader now, and I don't know that I'm prepared for a role this large.

Dreyden makes running Fire Court look like a breeze. Even though he is gone six days a week, everything still runs smoothly. The power and respect he holds keep his people in line, but will these lost fae hold me to the same level? How will we house this many people in Fire Court? How do I lead ten thousand people within his court?

If I were anyone else, he'd tell me to get lost, but he can't because I'm his mate. He'll give me the unfair advantage and be more lenient with me than he would with absolutely anyone else. Can I live with that?

I don't know.

But I'll have to figure it out as I go.

Dreyden sighs, reminding me I'm standing in the room with three other people and can't get lost in my own thoughts for longer than a few seconds. "We have enough food to get us through a little while, but we'll need to come up with some other means of meeting their needs if they're going to be here longer than a couple of weeks."

"Do you think they'll be ready to leave in a few weeks?" I ask him.

He shrugs as he raises his brows. "We'll have to see how it goes and adjust our plans according to what they're doing. Once their memory returns, they'll need to leave Fire Court. We can't support this many people."

Instant dread drags itself through my heart, and his words feel wrong. "We can't force them to leave. Where will they go?"

"I don't think that's our problem." His words are cold, like ice against the back of my neck from where he stands.

"It sure feels like my problem," I snap, looking toward the stars swirling on my arm. "I'm not leaving them."

He watches me, unsure how to proceed from here. He's mulling over his response, carefully choosing his next words. "You've chosen to over-exhaust yourself instead of processing the grief you're experiencing. Denial only works for so long, Adeena."

I stare at him, anger flowing from me in the form of fire at my fingertips, a bad habit I picked up from none other than my mate himself.

"We'll check on the progress being made outside," Izan says quietly as he stands from the table. "Let's go," he waves his hand toward Lyra.

Lyra rises from her chair without saying a word. She follows Izan out of the room, and they close the door quietly behind them.

Dreyden is standing dangerously close to me as fire flickers from my fingertips. I turn around to meet his glare, and we're nearly standing nose to nose.

"You're smothering me and it's the only way to get away from you."

His hard glare turns soft as my words strike their target. "I'm away in Tartarus all the time. I don't know how I can possibly give you more space than that."

I shake my head as I look down, my eyes landing on his chest. "I don't need that kind of space. You don't allow me to make decisions for myself, and you're constantly hovering over everything that I do. You may be bonded to me by the gods, but you are not the one in charge of my life. *I am*."

He closes his eyes, inhaling a deep breath, then slowly exhales it as he says, "It feels as though you're pushing me away, and this is my natural way of responding. I'm not doing it on purpose, but what do you expect from me when I feel like my mate is rejecting me?"

Rejecting him? Is that what he thinks I'm doing?

The flames lighting my fingertips recede back into my skin as my heart sinks and I realize how hurt he's feeling.

He reaches for my chin, holding it between his thumb and index finger, drawing my eyes back to his as he speaks. "I want and *need* to be there for you, Adeena. I can't let you slip away."

Resting my hand on his chest, I feel his heart pounding against me.

The heart that was *made* for me. The heart that was *chosen* for me. The heart that I can't let slip away either, not after everything we've been through and every bit of emotion I've felt for him since the second I laid eyes on him.

Our bond has always been there, and I'm not sure there's anything strong enough to break it. He's the air I breathe, and I know I can't live without him. I won't survive without him.

His heart beats strongly beneath my hand, and I feel the power he holds flowing through us like an electric current.

"You're not losing me," I whisper. "I am sorry I've made you feel like I'm pushing you away. That was never my intention, but I need you to understand that I accept your support and decline your criticism."

He nods, resting his forehead against mine so our noses are touching. "I can do that. I just need you to be careful."

"I am, but at the end of the day, I'll do what I have to if it means I'm protecting those I love. You need to trust that I'll make the right call if the time comes."

My brief death in Tartarus will scar him for life, but I hope he finds a way to come to terms with how I choose to live my life. Our world is dangerous and he can't shield me from everything. It would be unfair for both of us to live in constant paranoia. That's not how I want to spend my time in this second life that I've been given. I refuse to be weakened by the fear of the unknown.

The air is sucked from my lungs as he skims my bottom lip with his. "And I need to remind *you* that I will do whatever it takes to keep *you* safe."

"I know," I breathe through shallow breaths as his thumb strokes my jawline.

"Do you?" he growls against my lips and he holds my face. "Do you know that I will burn this entire world down to protect you? I will devote every ounce of my being to ensuring your happiness does not waiver, and I will destroy anything that gets in my way."

I quietly laugh, scoffing as I expose my teeth with a wickedly amused smile. "What if I'm standing in the way of my own happiness?"

His eyes darken as he plays along with my game. "Then I'll have to break you."

Chills roll down my spine, making my breath catch as my head tips backward. His hand catches the back of my head as it falls, firmly holding me in place while his lips crash against mine.

A hungry moan rises in his throat, vibrating against my mouth as I open for him, granting him the entry he seeks. His tongue is hot as it takes possession of my mouth, dominating my entire airway as he sucks me down. I grip his bicep as I rise to my toes, trying to find the smallest whisper of air between tongue lashings, but he's the one in control of my breathing. *He* decides when I take my next breath.

Adrenaline courses through my blood, twisting me into a euphoric high as he suffocates me. He sucks my bottom lip between his teeth, biting down with enough force to make it hurt but not quite hard enough to draw blood.

Gasping, I fill my lungs with as much air as he'll allow.

A devilish smirk crosses his lips as he moves his focus to my backside. His hands squeeze my ass, lifting me off the ground with ease. He pulls my legs toward him, wrapping them around his waist so that I'm pressing against the rapidly hardening cock caged inside his trousers.

I rock myself against his bulge, using the friction to relieve some of the pressure building in my core. A moan slips through my lips as guides my hips up and down, jerking me against him.

"Get on your knees," he barks as he suddenly drops me, putting a pause to my incoming orgasm.

I don't hesitate as my feet hit the floor, and I drop to my knees. I look up at him through doe-eyes, patiently waiting for him to free his massive cock from his tightening trousers. My mouth begins to water at the glorious sight as he pulls it out, then begins bouncing it off my soft lips, giving it a few quick strokes.

"Suck it," he commands with the most handsomely feral look on his face.

My lips part, opening as he guides his cock into my mouth. His eyes are molten and dark, swirling with desire as he watches me on my knees.

"Mmm," I moan, sending vibrations through him.

His body twitches at the intense pleasure, plunging his cock down my throat as he groans, "Fuck, baby. You know how much I love when you do that."

Smiling with my eyes, I spread my tongue flat against his length. I salivate as I slide my tongue all around his cock, preparing it to be stroked and ridden. I wrap my hand around the base of his cock, holding it in place as I slip it back into my mouth, taking him deeper and deeper as my throat loosens up.

His hands lace themselves through my hair, but he leaves me in control of the pace. His moans get louder as I begin stroking him with my hand, perfectly matching the speed I'm maintaining with my mouth. In unison, my hand and my mouth take him down my throat. Tightening around my hair, his fingers yank at my scalp as his pleasure intensifies. A sharp pain shoots across my head as he pulls, and I open my mouth to yelp, but he cuts me off as he lifts me off the ground, throwing me onto the conference table.

I use my elbows to sit up, pushing my back off the conference table to look at him. He growls a warning as he presses his hand against my chest, shoving me back against the table.

"Lay down and relax. You need to save your energy because after this you're going to ride my cock like the good girl I know that you are," he says as he tugs off my tight trousers, taking my thong with it.

Goosebumps rise over my skin, heightening my senses as his hands spread my legs.

This time he's the one to drop to his knees, falling to the floor as he licks up my inner thigh. He blows cool air across the trail of saliva, sending chills rattling through me.

I grip my tunic tightly as my back arches off the table. The anticipation of waiting for his tongue to reach my center makes heat pool between my legs, and I can feel myself getting wetter as he inches closer.

Pressing my legs flat against the table, he dives in. A sharp breath escapes my lips as he surprises me with the quickest flick of his tongue over my clit. His tongue slides up and down my center, burring itself between my folds. Dipping his thumb into my arousal, he raises it to my clit, and then begins to rub in tight, wet circles while he continues lapping his tongue over my flesh.

The pressure builds deep inside me, driving me dangerously close to the edge of insanity.

"Please don't stop," I cry out as I fall into a world of sweet ecstasy.

He keeps his pace consistent as I begin seeing stars, screaming out for more. There's a predatory look in his eye as he watches me come for him.

My head falls back and my mouth opens when I can't take any more, and suddenly he's standing before me, lining his cock up against me. He doesn't waste time slamming his cock inside me as deep as it'll go. I cry out again as I scratch at his forearms braced on both sides of me.

He swoops his arm under the small of my back, pulling my body off the table as he continues pumping in and out of me. I wrap my arms around his neck as he lifts me into a sitting position, and now I'm straddling him while he fucks me.

A chair scratches against the ground as he kicks it, repositioning it before he sits in it. He allows his body to fall into the chair, landing with a thud that slams his cock inside me. I reposition my knees on both sides of his hips, then begin bouncing up and down.

"That's it," he groans, meeting my exceedingly loud volume as I quicken my pace. "Take what's yours." His head tips back, resting against the top of the massive chair.

And I do.

I rise and fall over his cock with my hands wrapped around his neck, scratching at his skin as my pleasure builds. My breath turns to panting as my body goes into overdrive. My skin feels like fire at each one of his dominating touches, and sweat rolls down my back as I exhaust myself.

My stars begin shining, dancing across my arms as Dreyden and I fall into a luxurious high together.

His hands grip my ass, providing aid as my legs begin to tire. He slams me down on his cock as hard as he can, and I cry out each time I land. We're moving so fast I can barely breathe, and my pussy clenches his cock as I begin to come for the second time.

He's not far behind, and he lets out a terrifying roar as he comes with me.

Chapter Thirteen

DREYDEN

"I promise," Adeena smiles the most beautiful smile as she pushes me out the castle doors.

Turning to meet her sterling eyes, I sigh as I run my hands through my hair. "I mean it, Adeena. Do not overwork yourself while I'm gone. Lean on Izan and Lyra when you need to. They're here to help you."

I'm leaving for Tartarus again this morning after skipping out on Alaric the last two days. He received my messages about my delay and while he wasn't happy about it, he said he understood why I needed to remain in Fire Court longer than planned.

"How much damage could I do to myself in three days?" Adeena laughs as she grabs ahold of my hand, swinging it through the morning sunshine between us.

Raising my eyebrow at her, I warn, "Just be careful."

Three days away from Fire Court is more than enough time to do some serious damage if she's not careful, but I'm working on trusting her after our breakthrough conversation a couple of days ago. Plus, I have a lot of catching up to do in Tartarus. Two and a half days have passed since Alaric and I did our last supply drop, and we know the people are starving. It's time to get back out there and make up for lost time.

Alaric has had extra time to heal and should be ready to go as soon as I get there.

"Be careful," Adeena says as she pulls me into the sweetest hug, reminding me of the love Alaric and Ellia share.

"You too," I whisper as I kiss the top of her head.

The last two days have been peaceful. A sudden calm has washed over us and there seems to be a better sense of understanding now that we've had an open conversation. Both of us have had more patience than normal, which has led to zero disagreements... something we haven't experienced for months, and that's saying a lot considering there are ten thousand amnesic strangers staying in a campsite on my lawn.

She steps back, watching me through those stunning silver eyes as I open a blazing hot portal beside us.

I make brief eye contact with Izan on the other side of my portal just before I step through it. We nod in unison, silently agreeing he'll take care of Adeena while I'm gone.

I don't know what I would do without Izan. He ensures my time away from Fire Court runs smoothly, and I never have to worry about whether he has total control over every situation that arises.

"I'll be fine!" Adeena throws her hands up and scoffs as she watches the silent communication going on between me and Izan.

Shaking my head, I laugh at her frustration as I step through the portal. She knows I can't help it. Her safety is my number one priority whether she likes it or not. I can learn to give her some space, but I won't risk her safety in the process.

I filled our bed chambers with my butterfly spies while she ate breakfast this morning. She'll be surprised to find them sometime later today. They're her only way of communicating with me quickly if something were to happen in Fire Court while I'm gone. I don't foresee anything going wrong, but I secretly hope she sends me visions of her nude body. She did it once when I was away for a few days, and I couldn't get back to Fire Court fast enough. She teased me the entire time I was gone, sending visions of her perky breasts while she played with herself.

My cock hardens as violent winds whip past me inside the portal. Adeena struggled to keep her balance as a human in my portals, but now, as a fae, she's graceful as she walks through the hurricane winds.

Alaric's face comes into view as I step out of the portal, and my cock instantly goes soft.

"What's that look for?" Alaric asks as he clutches his hand over his heart, pretending to have hurt feelings.

I roll my eyes, not wanting to tell him that I had a hard cock the entire way here. "I was hoping Ellia would be standing here with a pan full of cinnamon rolls, but here you are," I lie.

There's an amused twinkle in his eyes, and it's easy to see he's feeling much better than when I left him two and a half days ago. He looks mostly healed, and his walk is strong as he crosses his yard. On a typical day, Alaric is stir-crazy, and I can't even imagine how much it bothered him to be stuck here while I was in Fire Court.

"It's nice to see you, too," he grins as I close the portal, opening my pocket portal beside our supply cart.

Razvan appears in the doorway to the house, and the widest smile spreads across his face as he sees me. "Dreyden!" he shouts as he bolts out the door, running in my direction. "You're back!"

His young man-boy body slams into me as he embraces me in the biggest hug. His arms wrap around me tightly as he lets out a content sigh. I fold my arms around him, hugging him back as I say, "Hey, buddy. How have you been while I've been gone?"

I'm not one for hugs, but Razvan holds a special place in my heart. I've watched him continue to be a light in the darkness as Tartarus deteriorates, and I couldn't be more proud of him. He helps without being asked, and he's always begging to do more.

Razvan steps back, looking toward the supplies Alaric is unloading into the supply cart. "I've been okay. There was a sphynx in the woods yesterday and we had to stay in the house all day. Did you bring any herb mixes? Mother wants to make meat sauce to can and store on the shelves."

My eyes land on Alaric as he confirms Razvan's words with a grim look. I glance down at Razvan, smiling as I answer him. "There should be a few different kinds in the spice bag. Take it to your mother, then bring the bag to the supply cart once she's done with it."

"I'll be fast!" Razvan beams as he snatches the bag from the pocket portal, running inside the house as quickly as his legs will carry him.

Rubbing the back of my neck, I walk toward Alaric. "A sphynx? You're sure?"

He exhales an excessively long, stressed sigh. "Yes." He throws another heavy bag into the supply cart, and the wheels groan under the weight. "It was spotted walking the edge of the forest about half a mile down the road. Looked like it was hunting."

Dread fills me as I imagine the damage a sphynx could do to the few remaining people of this village. Sphynxes are the result of dark magic gone wrong thousands of years ago. They'd been banished to the Wychwood Forest, and we haven't heard of any leaving the forest... until now.

"Did it attack anyone?" I ask.

He shakes his head. "No. Not that I've heard of, but I don't like how closely it's hunting around the village. It'll move in once it realizes we're an easy meal."

He's not wrong. A sphynx could hunt and kill every remaining person in this village in less than a week. "After our supply drop, I'm going to the woods to track it."

"I'll go with you," he says without missing a beat.

"No, you won't. You'll stay here with your wife and children. It's too dangerous out there and I will have a hard time protecting you against a sphynx. I can't risk it."

"I'm no good being stuck at the house," he argues.

My voice turns cold as I straighten my posture. "You're no good dead, Alaric. You have a family here that needs you. Tartarus needs you. You're too valuable to put in harm's way if it's not necessary."

He looks like he's going to argue, then stops himself. "Do you think you can take it on by yourself?"

I unload the last two bags into the supply cart, then close the pocket portal. "I don't see another option."

I'VE BEEN HUNTING this sphynx for three damn days, and I'm finally closing in.

It took him this long to make one fatal mistake, leading me straight to him. He stopped at the creek to drink early this morning, and I caught his lion-shaped track in the mud. From there, I was able to pick up a scent trail, and now he's so close I can feel the magic seeping from his pores.

A twig snaps in the distance as I creep forward. My ears twitch as I zero in on the exact direction of the sound.

I suspect he knows I'm hunting him, and that's why I've had such a hard time tracking him. Sphynxes are notoriously smart, making them nearly impossible to find if they want to remain hidden.

My foot catches on a vine as I step over a log, causing me to stumble forward. I wince, holding my breath as my foot lands with a loud thud against the damp forest floor.

A dark, sickening laugh rings out somewhere ahead of me, making the hair on the back of my neck rise. It echoes off the trees around me, and I find myself looking in every direction as his laugh gets louder.

Eagle wings come into sight first, maybe a hundred feet ahead of me, and then I see his human head. His tanned skin and black eyes are a dark contrast to the light shade of fur covering his lion-shaped body. A pearly white smile crosses his face as he confidently stalks toward me.

His voice sends shivers down my spine as it roars through the dimly lit forest. "You found me quicker than I anticipated. I was beginning to enjoy our reversed cat and mouse game."

Sphynxes are sneaky and unpredictable, so I watch him with caution, waiting for him to make a move. "And what makes you think I'm the mouse?" I calmly question as a sly smile exposes my teeth.

Amusement flickers in his eyes as I challenge his judgment. "I have roamed this world for ten thousand years. I have faced far more than a stupidly brave lone fae."

Unfortunately for him, he doesn't know who I am, and he is clueless to the extent of the power I hold. He can sense that I am fae, and he can very likely feel my power, but he isn't prepared for my dark storm.

"A stupid mouse, you say?" I raise my brow, folding my hands behind my back, silently lighting fire across each fingertip. My magic inches closer to the surface of my skin as I call it, balling it up as I begin poking at his mind with my words. "What will the people say when they find out the ancient sphynx was killed by a mere mouse?"

The amusement dims in his eyes, and he's quickly angered by my insult. "You're more foolish than I have given you credit for."

"Perhaps," I laugh as I take a step toward him. "But I'm not going to die today."

Fire lights in his eyes as he lunges for me, using his lion speed to propel his body toward me at lightning speed. "YOU FOOL," he roars, sending a blast of energy toward the trees around us. Several trees crack, booming a thunderous sound as they fall to the ground.

I remove my hands from my back, exposing what I've built during our brief conversation. Planting my legs against the ground, I steady my stance as I wind my arm back, then throw a ball of fire energy at him.

He's too fast, and he swerves around my ball of fire as he barrels toward me. The distance between us closes too quickly, and he's knocking me off my feet before I can even think. My back hits the ground with enough force to kill a human, and I wince in pain. He's on top of me, pawing at my neck as he pins me down. A sharp pain slices through my chest as he swats at me, forcing me to yell out in both pain and anger.

His paws shapeshift, turning into oversized human hands as he wraps them around my neck, cutting off my air supply. In the ancient language, "sphynx" translates to "strangler," and he's staying true to his roots.

A wicked laugh sprays cold spit over my face as he gets off to strangling me. The weight of his lion body pressing down on me hurts more than I'd like to admit. I feel like I'm suffocating more from the pressure of his body than the hands wrapped around my neck.

"Get. Off. Me," I grunt as I grip his forearms, pushing against him.

A thick purple vein in his forehead pops out as he tightens his grip around my neck, pressing into me with all his strength.

I need to think fast. This mutant cat bastard will not get the best of me today; he just doesn't know it yet. I call my power to my hands again as I struggle, charging up for an electric shock that'll send this cat bastard flying into the air.

There's a crazed look in his black eyes, and I know this is the last thing each one of his victims has seen as they've died. It sickens me to know he gets this much enjoyment out of killing. He should never have been sent to the Wychwood Forest. He should have been killed long before being exiled.

Digging my nails into his wrists, I release the energy I've been building.

His body goes stiff as I deliver my shot, sending him flying like a scaredy-cat as he screeches in pain. The fur on his body sticks straight up as my energy flows through him, and the smell of burnt hair hits my nose.

I inhale, filling my lungs with air as he recovers from my shock. Sitting up, I rub my neck where his hands had previously been. "That wasn't very nice," I say coolly as I rise to my feet, brushing myself off. Warm liquid flows down my cheek, and I know I'm bleeding badly.

His face is feral and dark as he watches me from a short distance. "You're going to regret that."

My lips twitch, turning up on one side as I allow my true self to show. Fire lights along my fingertips one finger at a time. The stars branded across my skin begin to shine through the fabric concealing them. "That's no way to talk to the high lord of Fire Court."

There's a moment of silence between us as his face shifts. The wild animalistic side of him fades, and fear overwhelms him as he watches me. He takes a step back, and I match his step as I walk forward with a smile on my face.

"I'll leave," he begs. "I'll go back to the Wychwood Forest, and I won't return. "You have my word."

"Tsk," I shake my head. "Sphynxes are notorious for lying."

He continues walking backward as I stalk forward at the same pace, feeding the fire within my hands. "I'm not. You'll never see me again."

"The only way to ensure I never see you again is to kill you." My voice is cold and hollow, emotionless, and numb.

His face pales, and he suddenly turns to run. Before he can fully face his back to me, I send a massive ball of fire toward him. He screams out as he falls to the ground, hissing in pain while it engulfs his entire body in flames. Black smoke fills the air around us, and I nearly gag at his putrid odor. Rolling and tossing himself over the ground, he tries to put out the flames before they can eat him alive.

Bloodcurdling screams fill my ears as I force the fire to stay lit, fueling it with my magic. "Your death was decided the second you stepped foot out of the Wychwood Forest."

Chapter Fourteen

"What made you think stealing would be okay?" I ask the three young fae boys standing before me.

Early this morning, the three boys snuck down to Phenix and found their way through the market, stealing whatever they wanted along the way. Outraged villagers stormed to the castle shortly after the boys left, demanding compensation for the stolen items. Several of them were nearly screaming at Izan as they carried on about how justice needs to be served and that the lost fae should be removed from Fire Court.

Their frustration is justifiable, and I don't blame them for being angry. I'm upset myself. The entire group of lost fae has been told over and over again to not leave the legion camp, and this is the sixth incident since Dreyden left three days ago.

Lyra, Izan, and I keep putting out the fires, but we're all exhausted and mentally drained. I feel like an absolute failure. If I can't keep control of them for three days without Dreyden, how am I supposed to lead these people and help them gain traction in their new lives? How are they supposed to look at me as their high lady when I can't even keep track of a group of children?

Some of the lost travelers feel trapped, enraged even, being forced to stay here, but it's the best way to ensure their safety from what lies beyond the castle grounds and to keep them separated from the Fire Court people. We can't have strangers wandering around Fire Court when we don't know their entire story.

The oldest boy has a smug look on his face as he watches me. His thin lips are sealed, and he hasn't said a word the entire time they've been in the castle.

It's the youngest boy who speaks first. His silver eyes flicker as he finds his voice. "We're sick of eating the same things over and over again. We wanted some real food."

A handful of children showed up with the lost fae, and none of them have parental supervision, so we've all been pitching in to make sure they're taken care of. Edlynne keeps an eye on them most of the time, but she's struggling to keep up with their troubled outbursts. They're old enough to know better, and that makes it even more frustrating.

"You eat the same food repeatedly so that we do not run out of food for you," Izan snaps, his eyes dark and hard as he speaks to them. "There are limited resources when there are ten thousand mouths to feed. You should be grateful you are being fed at all. Would you prefer we let you starve? Would that make you happy?"

I fold my arms over my chest, waiting for the boys to respond.

They're frightened of Izan and it's easy to see why. He towers over them by nearly two feet, not to mention he's solid muscle. If looks could kill, these boys would be dead.

"We're sorry," the middle boy mumbles as he looks to the ground, avoiding eye contact with me.

"What?" I ask sharply, quickly running out of patience. "I couldn't hear you."

"We're sorry," he repeats, louder this time as he raises his eyes to mine.

Nodding his head as he glances between me and Izan, the youngest boy agrees. "We're sorry, High Lady. It won't happen again."

"You're damn right it won't happen again," Izan cuts in. "You're on dish duty for the rest of the week. You will immediately relieve the group assigned to dish duty and the three of you will do ALL the dishes yourselves."

Leaning forward as he throws scrawny his scrawny arms up, the oldest boy decides now is the time to argue. "But-"

"But *nothing*," I cut him off. "You will do as you are told or there will be further consequences. This is your final warning. This will be a very different discussion if we must have it again."

Two days ago, this same group of boys snuck down the path leading into the Bloodred Forest and started a small fire. The legion had to work quickly to get it put out before it spread larger than it already had, which is ironic considering this is Fire Court. I thought they would have a better hold on the concept of fire, but amid the chaos I learned they do *not*.

"The villagers are angry," Lyra snaps. "You're wearing out your welcome *very* quickly. We would like to find a place for you, but you need to prove your value to us. Do not cause more trouble than what you are worth. Be better than that."

The boys nod as their faces fall in shame.

"Dish duty begins now," I say as I wave them away.

"Yes, High Lady," they say in unison as they bow, then scurry out of Dreyden's office.

Izan closes the door behind them once they're out of the room. "This is becoming too much, Adeena," he sighs. "When Dreyden gets back to see all of this, he's not going to be happy."

"I know," I groan, frustrated with the lack of control I've maintained with Dreyden being gone.

The lost fae are deeply troubled by their memory loss, and they're acting out in response to the confusion. Most of them are doing fine and haven't been any trouble, but there are too many beginning to create chaos.

"Brina hasn't left the garden since they trampled through it," Lyra sighs.

She's just as exhausted as Izan and I are. We've barely slept since Dreyden left. We're trying to keep over ten thousand lost and confused fae confined, happy, and fed while also maintaining peace with the Fire Court people.

It's tough, and right now it's feeling next to impossible.

"The broken windows should be fixed before Dreyden gets back, but we're going to have to tell him," Izan says. He's looking at me with a sternness in his face, and I know there's no arguing with him.

I nod slowly, not wanting to agree. "I know. I don't know what else to do with all these people."

Izan's voice is stone-cold and serious. "They're going to have to leave. There isn't another option. We do not have the resources to keep up with ten thousand fae, and if they're causing trouble, then they're not adding any value to Fire Court. The Fire Court people do not want them here, and for good reason. They're breaking windows, starting fires, and stealing food. What's next?" He throws his hands in the air. "Muggings? Murders?"

"No," I snap, matching his icy tone. "There will be no muggings or murders. I'll be sure of it."

"How can you be sure? They're impossible to control."

Tears form in the back of my eyes, and I choke down spit as I swallow the lump caught in my throat. I don't know whether I should be excited or worried for Dreyden to get home in a few short hours. Perhaps he can help get things under control... but he's more likely to side with Izan, and he already strongly dislikes the lost fae.

Chapter Fifteen

DREYDEN

I huff as I walk down the halls of my castle. Adeena is going to be so pissed off when she sees the deep gashes in my face and neck gifted to me by the sphynx, and I'm not in the mood to deal with her lectures about being safe.

Perhaps it's a bit hypocritical, but I can take care of myself. I did what I had to, and it was a stupid slip in judgment when the sphynx had me pinned to the ground. I should have known he would be fast as fuck, but in the end, I'm the one who walked away, and that cat bastard burned to the ground as a pile of ash.

Adeena doesn't know I'm back yet, and I'd like to keep it that way until I'm finished meeting with Izan about Fire Court business. We need to discuss our food supplies, water resources, village politics, and everything else we've been avoiding like the plague.

I don't know how much longer we can keep feeding these people. I don't have an exact count, but we estimated around ten thousand lost travelers the day they arrived. Fire Court is self-sufficient for its own people, but ten thousand throws us off balance. Our numbers nearly double in size with the addition of that many people. There's a secret reserve very few people know about, but I refuse to tap into it for anyone other than the Fire Court people. We've been building it for years, canning and preserving food items with magic to last us as long as possible if a crisis were to occur. Something like what's happening in Tartarus, but Tartarus did not have a backup plan.

Izan waits for me in my office, patiently seated in the large leather chair across from my desk. His enormous binder full of notes and important information is in his hands, and he's scanning through it with his leg crossed over his knee.

He hears me walk into the room, and glances up from his binder. "What happened to you? You look like you got into a fight with a cat."

I scoff, quietly laughing as I cross the room to my desk. He's not far off. "A sphynx."

His back straightens, and he slams his binder shut as he sits forward. "A sphynx? I haven't heard of anyone running into a sphynx in hundreds of years."

"Well, there are all sorts of creatures that no one has seen for hundreds of years freely running around Tartarus right now. I took care of the sphynx as soon as I heard it was spotted near town."

"We need to do something about that," Izan says as he rubs his hand over his chin. "They can't take over an entire kingdom."

"I've already tried getting the other courts on board, but no one wants to use their resources on a fallen kingdom."

Izan sits deep in thought, mulling over some options. "There has to be a way to change their minds."

I sit at my desk across from him, picking up a pen and straightening a pile of papers. "Let me know if you come up with anything. I've been through it a thousand times in my mind."

AFTER MY MEETING WITH IZAN, I find Adeena standing outside with the lost travelers, mingling among them. She's wearing her usual black trousers and black tunic. I secretly love how similarly she dresses to me.

I approach her from behind, following the sweet vanilla and jasmine scent I love so much. She jumps in surprise as I wrap my arms around her waist, pulling her close to me. Her hand lands on my forearm as she prepares to tear free of my grasp.

"It's me," I whisper into her ear as I bury my face in her long blonde hair, inhaling her scent.

She immediately relaxes at the sound of my voice, melting into my arms. "I missed you," she breathes, leaning against me while I hold her weight.

Her head falls back against my chest, landing on one of my deep wounds. I wince in pain as silently as I can, but she notices me flinch. She turns toward me faster than I can stop her. I knew this was coming.

I kiss her cheek as she rotates toward me, stalling her for another second. "I missed you too."

Her sterling eyes fill with concern as they land on the deep cuts covering my face and neck. Raising her hand to my cheek, she slides a finger just below a cut. "What happened?"

She looks like she wants to cry seeing me hurt, and it breaks my heart. I'm fine, but explaining that to her is easier said than done.

"I got into a fight with a cat," I shrug with a gentle smile, running my thumb and index finger under her chin, tipping her lips to meet mine as I plant a soft kiss.

"I can see that," she says, avoiding my gaze as she surveys the gashes in my flesh. "What cat would do this to you?"

Considering my options for a moment, I decide I shouldn't lie to her. I'm working on trusting her, and I can't break her trust in the process, even if she won't like my answer. "There was a sphynx hunting near Northford. I took care of it before it made its way into town."

She pales at my mention of the creature. "I thought sphynxes were a myth."

Shaking my head, I say, "They're not a myth. There are a few that have dwelled within the Wychwood Forest for hundreds of years. The Archai courts and Tartarus exiled them instead of killing them. Probably a stupid mistake now that I think back on it."

"Is Tartarus livable anymore?" she asks.

A question I've thought through many times before. "The truth is, I don't know. If we can find a way to take control of the criminals and creatures it could be made livable again with some time. If we can't rid Tartarus of the evils... the few remaining people will not survive. Not for much longer. The supply drops are being cleared out shortly after we're stocking them. We can't keep up."

"They need a leader," she sighs, looking deep into my eyes.

I nod, closing my eyes as she strokes the back of my neck, slowly massaging the store muscles. "They need a leader and a large show of force to round up the criminals and scare the creatures back into the Wychwood Forest."

She's quiet as she continues massaging, kneading her fingers into my neck. There's a light tingle that zips along the surface of my skin, raising every hair on my body for a brief second. I open my eyes to find her glowing with a soft silver aura surrounding her body.

"What are you doing?" I ask, my voice barely a whisper as I watch her in awe. "I've never seen you do this."

She smiles sweetly as she removes her hand from my neck and the aura around her dims. "I told you I've been working on some things."

I feel around, chasing the tingle on my neck and face as it fades with her aura, and I realize my wounds are gone. "You healed me," I gasp with wide eyes.

She stands there beaming at me, quietly waiting for the praise she knows is coming.

"Perhaps your training sessions aren't as bad as I thought. You've learned so much from Geras. He's teaching you these tricks faster than I learned them... It took me *years* to master the art of healing, and sometimes I'm still not the best at it."

Her eyes light up as she whispers against my lips, "It's nice to hear you admit when you're wrong."

"I'm doing my best to trust that you know best," I wink at her, stealing a quick kiss as she grins at me.

Pulling her into a hug, I wrap my arms around her tightly as she hugs me back. I rest my chin on the top of her head.

For the first time since arriving home, I take a second to look around. There's a line of travelers arriving toward the end of the row we're standing in.

"They're still arriving? How many?" I ask as I pull back to meet Adeena's eyes.

She's reluctant to answer my question, and there's hesitation in her voice. "We don't know the exact number, but I'm estimating we're over twelve thousand now."

"I think we need to finish our meeting with Izan and Lyra."

Exhaling deeply, she nods in agreement. "Yes, I know. I've already set it up for this evening. They've cleared their schedules to meet with us after dinner."

Chapter Sixteen

ADEENA

Lyra and Izan walk into Dreyden's office together, laughing and smiling as they talk. Lyra's laugh is contagious as she enters the room, and I can't help but grin seeing her so happy and carefree for the first time in days. There haven't been any incidents since the three boys stole items at the market this morning, and we've all had a chance to breathe.

They take their seats in their usual spots at the conference table. Dreyden and I are already sitting at the table. We arrived a few minutes ago after having a quiet dinner on the edge of the cliffs overlooking the Bloodred Forest.

Izan opens his binder and then picks up his pen, ready to take notes. "Here's to hoping this meeting goes better than the last," he points his pen between Dreyden and me with a stern look.

Dreyden watches him in silence, probably trying to decide if he should make a smart-ass comment or not.

In the end, he decides to get down to business without wasting any time. "We need to talk about the lost fae."

Immediately making my stance clear, I say, "We need to find a way to help them. They're still confused and they're feeling lost emotionally in addition to *actually* being lost."

Dreyden's voice is suddenly cold, the polar opposite of what I experienced at dinner a few moments ago. "Fire Court resources are already being stretched thin between Fire Court and the supply drops I make in Tartarus. We can't afford to feed this many people. It's not practical."

My stomach drops. He's not here to mess around.

"What else are they supposed to do? We can't just send them away. It's not safe for them out there. There have to be some more resources here we can tap into."

Izan scoffs across from me, rolling his eyes as he mumbles, "They're already taking whatever they want."

Dreyden's head snaps in Izan's direction as I shoot Izan a warning glare. "What?" he asks, looking between me and Izan, confused as to what we're talking about.

"Tell him," Izan says as he crosses his arms, leaning back in his chair. "You can't hide it forever."

The plan wasn't to hide it forever, just delay it for a short time until I figured out what to do.

I swallow hard, not wanting to have this conversation with Dreyden while Izan and Lyra are here with us. "There was a small incident with a few of the younger boys while you were gone, but I took care of it and it's no longer a problem."

"You're being too protective of them," Izan laughs as he uncrosses his arms, throwing them in the air. "They're causing problems and stirring up trouble. The villagers are *mad* and feel disrespected by these 'lost' travelers. We chased them around the entire time you were gone. They're out of control."

Anger bubbles under my skin as I try to stay calm. This isn't how I wanted to tell him. Izan doesn't give a shit about the lost travelers, and I'm fairly certain he'd do anything to get rid of them at this point.

"Then it's settled," Dreyden's voice booms across the table as his patience wears thin. "They need to leave. We'll get them sent on their way in the morning. They can rest tonight, but they're gone once the sun comes up. That's more than enough if they're disrespecting my people. I won't tolerate it. You had all day to bring this to my attention, Adeena, and you failed to do so. This leads me to believe you don't care for the people of Fire Court like I do."

My heart begins to pound in my chest, my stomach dropping as his words roll off his tongue. They can't leave. They're protected up here, by the castle. I can't control the environment for them outside of this safe space. It'd be cruel to make them leave. And how dare he accuse me of not caring? Is he joking?

My cheeks heat as I lose my patience with Dreyden. "They're not leaving. You're sentencing them to death if you send them out there! There's no telling what would happen to them! Some of them are children. You can't possibly be *that* cruel."

Perhaps this is the deadly high lord of Fire Court I've heard about over the years.

"I don't care," he says blatantly. "They need to leave. I won't sacrifice the people of Fire Court for these people we know nothing about. I don't care who they are or why they were sent here. They do not belong here."

"But-"

He cuts me off coldly, "But nothing, Adeena. This is not up for discussion. This is *my* court, these are *my* rules."

Disgust rolls through me as I snap my mouth shut.

How can he act like their lives don't matter? How can he pretend they aren't tied to me by a higher power, a higher power we need to *respect* and *trust?* His male dominance makes me feel sick to my stomach. He doesn't have this power over me.

I control my life, no one else. Not my friends, not my mate. I do.

Izan and Dreyden begin talking over plans to evacuate the lost fae first thing in the morning, and I tune them out as I think through my options. If their place isn't here, then my place isn't here either, and I need to plan accordingly.

"What about Tartarus?" I interrupt their intense conversation.

Dreyden turns toward me with a confused expression on his face. "What about Tartarus?"

"I'll take them to Tartarus," I breathe, unsure if this plan will actually work or not, but it feels right and I'm going for it.

Dreyden's eyes harden as he glares at me. "You'd leave with them? You'd choose the lost travelers over me?"

I shake my head as he puts words in my mouth. "No, I wouldn't *choose* them over you. You're in Tartarus all the time anyway, and you agreed that Tartarus needs a leader."

Something deep within Dreyden breaks, and I can feel the pain leaking from his heart.

Izan lets out a hysterical laugh, filling the entire room with his amusement. "*You* are going to take on Tartarus?" He wipes a tear from his waterline as his laughter calms. "Yeah, right."

"Why can't she?" Lyra says dryly toward Izan, speaking for the first time since we sat down for this meeting. "Adeena crumpled the Tartarus monarchy. Why shouldn't she be the one to rule?" She reaches for my hand resting on the table, grabbing hold of it as she looks into my eyes. "I'll go with you."

Now both Izan and Dreyden look hurt, bleeding internally as we make plans to leave them. I can't help but tear up as I watch my friend stand up for me. I grip tightly around her hand, holding onto it like my life depends on it.

"You'd leave Fire Court to go back *there?* You can't be serious." Izan asks, painful sadness seeping from his voice.

"I am serious," she nods. "Wherever Adeena goes, I go. We've been through it all together, and I refuse to stop now."

I smile at my beautiful, confident, and supportive friend. The best friend I've always wanted but never had.

Until now.

She's my ride-or-die, and she's a fucking queen.

I straighten, glancing around the table of mixed emotions. I avoid Dreyden's gaze, already knowing how broken he's feeling. "Then it's settled. We'll take the lost fae to Tartarus."

Chapter Seventeen

DREYDEN

My world feels like it's crashing.

My heart feels like it's tired of beating.

And I feel like I'm dying.

Adeena's face is lit up, radiating confidence as she makes plans with Lyra to leave Fire Court and take on Tartarus. Izan and I are sitting here in deadly silence.

Absolute shock. Numb.

There's no other way to describe what I'm feeling right now. My mate has just declared her wish to part from our home and take on a new life in the world's most dangerous place with twelve thousand strangers.

Perhaps she's not in her right mind... Maybe I was right about her mental instability and this is her big breakdown.

The tidal wave I was waiting for.

She said I was smothering her, so I have taken a step back, but clearly, it hasn't been enough. What if... this is what she needs? What if this is how I can get her back?

She'll take one step into Tartarus and she'll be overwhelmed. She'll come running back to me after she realizes how horrible the conditions are over there. I just must keep her safe while she figures that out.

I owe it to her to let her try, but if this plan fails I don't know what I'll do. I don't know how I could live a life without her. My life is here in Fire Court. I have a duty to lead Fire Court. How would we ever make it work if she's on the other side of the continent?

I close my eyes, breathing in and out slowly to keep myself from panicking. Adeena's voice continues flowing around me, and I finally come back to reality, focusing on what she's saying.

I'll help her get the lost fae out of my court, and then I'll escort her home to safety when she realizes how difficult it will be to take control of Tartarus without the support of the other Archai courts.

PREPARATIONS TO LEAVE Fire Court have been going on for two days. Adeena has taken charge while I've stepped back, allowing her to have full control of the situation.

It's hard, but I know it's what I need to do if this plan is going to work.

Tomorrow morning the Fire Court legion will escort the lost fae to Tartarus. They'll be taken to Northford, where Alaric resides with his family. Most of the houses are empty there and the village is large enough to take on twelve thousand fae.

Surrounding villages are vacant as well, and they'll be easy to spread into if Northford becomes too crowded. The lost fae can't possibly make Tartarus any worse than it already is, but I don't know how Adeena plans on handling the food shortage. Twelve thousand mouths will not be easy to feed, and the supply drops can't handle that many people. The supply drops already can't handle the small number of people residing in Northford.

They'll have to learn to fend for themselves against looters. If they can stay alive long enough to learn how to fight they should have a solid chance at survival, considering most of the looters are human. As for the feral creatures roaming Tartarus... there's no telling what kind of damage they'll inflict upon the lost fae. It takes an experienced fighter to take on the creatures that have been locked within the borders of the Wychwood Forest for hundreds of years... and none of these people seem to have a clue what they're doing.

Adeena has been so busy the last two days I've barely seen her. Izan informed me she sent word to Hali, Soren, and Weylin, inviting them to Fire Court for a meeting that I am now on my way to. I already know how the meeting will go because I tried having the very same meeting with them months ago, and they weren't receptive to my ideas. No one wants to use their resources to clean up Tartarus without a reward, and Adeena has nothing to offer.

I'm the last to walk into my office, and I'm surprised to find everyone seated at the conference table, chatting and laughing like old friends. Hali and Adeena seem cozier than normal, and it almost makes me uncomfortable to see them together.

Perhaps that's because I don't believe my friendship with Hali can be salvaged... not after her poor response to my pleas for help aiding Tartarus. She turned her head just as quickly as the other two had, and it still disgusts me. I already feel sorry for Adeena. She's going to be lost for words when they deny her requests in the same way they did mine, smashing her newfound dream of ruling Tartarus. If anything, they'll laugh in her face when she asks.

I'll be here to comfort her, though. I'll be here to remind her how safe Fire Court is.

"Hali," I nod, my voice stale as I acknowledge her, taking my seat at the head of the table.

"Dreyden," she says quietly.

She *knows* we're not on good terms. I made it clear I wasn't happy with her when I stormed out of our last meeting. She hadn't even tried to come after me or fix things. She abandoned my requests because, as Alaric would put it, it didn't fit her "agenda."

Adeena clasps her hands together, somehow still holding onto the same enthusiasm she has expressed for the last two days.

It's exhausting.

She passes around some papers she worked on all morning, making copy after copy for each of the court rulers. I glance down at it, and I see that it's a detailed outline of her plans for Tartarus... plans far more extensive than I was expecting.

Adeena clears her throat before beginning, and everyone watches her as she captivates their interest. "I've asked you all here because I have plans to leave Fire Court with the twelve thousand lost fae released to me by the gods. We've quickly outgrown Fire Court, and there is no place for this many fae anywhere within Archai. We'll head to Tartarus, and once we're there I fully intend on taking over as the new ruler. As you all know, no one has stepped into a ruling position since the fall of Tartarus months ago." Her voice is stable and smooth as she speaks, commanding the attention of the court rulers. "We need to discuss the possibility of Tartarus joining the Archai courts. Four courts would become five. Land, wind, water, fire, and..."

"Sky," Hali breathes with a wild excitement in her eyes.

Adeena smiles at her as though they've been friends forever, making me nearly roll my eyes. "Yes," she nods. "Sky Court."

"You'd need your own legion," Weylin chimes in. "How will you keep your people protected in such a feral land?"

Already having an answer prepared, Adeena doesn't miss a beat. "I've already begun sending word across Tartarus to round up recruits. There is a sign-up form in the legion campground for the lost fae to use if they're interested. We've already gathered seven hundred names, and the list is quickly growing. These people *want* to go. They don't feel welcome here, and they're ready to start a new life, which is why we need to get them into Tartarus safely as soon as possible."

"How will you get them there? Surely Dreyden can't portal that many at once," Soren says, glancing between me and Adeena.

"I can't," I shake my head. "The plan is for the Fire Court legion to escort them through the Wychwood Forest. I don't see how the forest could be any more hazardous than Tartarus currently is, but we'll take them all the way to the village of Northford. I have contacts there already preparing for our arrival."

Yesterday I compiled messages for Alaric, letting him know we would be on our way there with twelve thousand people. I'm sure he's not happy about it, but I don't know what else to do. This will make Adeena the happiest until she realizes how horrible Tartarus is, then she'll come running home to me in

Fire Court and never want to leave again. The lost fae will be out of my court, and they'll have to figure out how to make Tartarus, or Sky Court, livable again.

The three other court rulers sit quietly with their eyes glued to the plan written out before them, reading over the words carefully. Adeena silently watches them, waiting for their response. She's fidgeting in her chair a little bit, and I can't tell she's nervous. Who wouldn't be?

She managed to gather all four of the Archai court rulers into one room with a one-day notice. It's nearly unheard of.

A few minutes pass without a word. Weylin twiddles with his chin while he reads, contemplating his options.

Hali gently sets the paper down and then turns to Adeena. "Your plan includes using Archai court teams to take control of the loose creatures. *If* we spare the resources, we expect them to be used properly."

My jaw nearly hits the floor.

Spare the resources?

Is she seriously considering this? After I spent months begging for help, she's *actually* thinking about sending a team of fighters into Tartarus to round up the loose creatures.

Weylin nods, "I agree. It's about time we get Tartarus... *Sky Court*," he corrects. "Under control. If each court sends in a team we should be able to secure the creatures within the month. The border will need to be maintained to make this effort worthwhile, but I don't have a problem sending in a team or two, especially if it means we gain an alliance with you, Adeena."

"I'm in," Hali announces, slapping her hand down on the conference table. "It'd be nice to have another high lady to keep these high lords in line."

I lean forward, barely breathing as I watch them. I'm struggling to even form words at this point.

"I am as well," Weylin beams. "You proved your worth and loyalty in the war with Tartarus, and that's more than enough for me. You died for us all. We owe *you*."

Soren finally looks up from the plan Adeena had written, and says, "This plan is very simple. It's cut and dry, but it'll work if we all pitch in. The addition of a court to our alliance is priceless. Wind Court will happily supply enough men to round up the loose creatures."

My heart is pounding in my ears and my stomach feels like it's in my throat. This isn't how I expected this meeting to go at all. I figured by the end of it Adeena would have tears in her eyes while the three of them pranced themselves back to their own little worlds, but here we are.

They're *all* offering Adeena assistance, and they're doing it with a smile on their faces.

"Dreyden?" Adeena asks with a softness in her voice.

I look up to find the four of them staring at me blankly. I must not have heard them say something.

"Yes?" I ask, clearing my throat as I come back to reality.

Adeena looks slightly concerned as she stares at me. "We want your final approval of the plan. We need to know if we're leaving in the morning."

My approval?

She doesn't have it, but she doesn't know that. I don't approve of any of this. How could the three of them offer so much support to Adeena after I've been begging them for months? Why is it so easy for *her* to convince them, but they wouldn't give me the time of day?

Not only that, but I can't willingly watch Adeena leave me. I can't aid her in her plan to move across the continent and live in the most dangerous place she could possibly find.

If the courts all send in teams to clean up Tartarus it could be made livable and safe much faster than I anticipated, and she might not want to come home to me. I can't live with that. I can't live without her.

I hesitate to answer her. There's a lump in my throat I can barely swallow as I watch her through panicked eyes. I hope the court rulers can't see straight through me right now. There's probably no concealing how I'm feeling.

They're all quiet as they wait for my answer. Their awkward silence makes me feel worse.

"Yes," I nod with a forced smile. "We will leave tomorrow morning with the lost fae and the Fire Court legion."

Vomit nearly comes out with the words as I say them. My stomach is twisting and turning inside me, and I feel disgustingly sick. A cold sweat breaks out across my forehead as I watch my mate. She's concerned, but she's not saying anything. She's giving me the "we'll talk about this later" look.

"Perfect," she grins a forced smile of her own, but the three other court rulers appear to be oblivious. "Sky Court will join Archai as the fifth court in the kingdom."

The four of them talk game plans and strategy for the next couple of hours, and I'm mostly silent as they plot. I'm feeling defeated and broken as I listen to my mate make plans to start a new life so far away from me. My duty to Fire Court keeps me here. I don't know how we could ever make a relationship work being so far away permanently. Temporarily, sure, but forever? It's not possible.

We would rarely sleep in the same bed. We would reside in two different homes, and have duties to our own kingdoms. And what if politics get in the way someday? Sure everything is fine now, but what about in the future? There's no way to know what the future of Archai will hold.

I feel ill.

I'm losing my mate.

———

As Adeena slips into my favorite silk robe for the night I can feel the heat and frustration radiating off her body. She hasn't said a word to me since the meeting ended earlier this afternoon, and I know it's because of how I reacted to the overwhelming support provided by the other courts.

She climbs into bed beside me without saying a word. She crosses her arms over her chest as she snuggles her head into the large pillow on her side of the bed. She's lying on her back, facing the ceiling with a blank expression on her face.

Her breathing is deeper than normal, and it's not hard to tell she's trying to maintain control of her anger. I watch her for a few minutes, contemplating whether I should say something.

This isn't how I want to spend her final night in Fire Court. She seems so okay with leaving this suddenly, and that's what breaks my heart the most. How can she be *this* okay with leaving me?

"How are we going to make this work?" I whisper, holding back tears before they can rise in my eyes.

She breaks her glare at the ceiling, glancing over at me. "I don't know why you're so worried about how we're going to make this work. You're in Northford six days a week anyway. If anything, we might see each other more often than we do now."

I sigh, running my fingers through my hair as I lay beside her. Perhaps this is why she isn't having a hard time coming to terms with the fact she's leaving me. She doesn't think she's leaving me.

"We will no longer go to bed together every evening. Do you know how much that breaks my heart, Adeena?" I prop myself up on an elbow, facing her as I rest the side of my head against my hand. "I don't know what I'll do without you."

Her cheeks turn red as frustration rises in her face. "Is this why you were so quiet at the meeting today? Do you realize you risked my entire plan by being so blatantly unsupportive in front of the court rulers?"

My stomach drops. We can't spend our final night together arguing. I can't do it. She'll never come home if her time in Fire Court ends like this, so I force myself to stay calm.

"I'm sorry," I apologize as I brush my fingers along her forearm, raising goosebumps across her soft skin. "I was taken by surprise when they were so supportive, and I reacted poorly. I'm afraid you'll never come back once you leave. You'll find a new life and forget about me as time passes. You won't need me if you're on the other side of the continent running your own court. To be honest, I'm terrified."

She turns on her side, matching how I lay beside her. "I could *never* forget about you, Dreyden. We are bonded by the gods, and there is no connection in the entire world stronger than that. We were made for each other. There's no breaking that."

"Then how can you leave me so easily?" The hurt is apparent in my voice.

Adeena sits up and then crawls to my side of the bed. I roll to my back as she climbs on top of me, straddling my hips as she looks down at me through sterling silver eyes.

"You think this is easy for me?" she asks, tears wallowing in her waterline. "I feel torn between the life I've loved living here with you, and the pull I'm feeling toward these helpless people. They *need* a leader. Tartarus *needs* a leader. Would it not be selfish for me to remain in lavish Fire Court comfort when I should be out there saving these people? Saving Tartarus? Is that not what you've been working at for months?"

I hadn't thought of it that way. My lips part as I'm lost for words.

How stupid could I be? How *selfish* could I be?

All this time I've only been thinking of myself and how Adeena leaving will affect me. Why couldn't I see past my own feelings and put others first? The world doesn't revolve around me, so why did I think Adeena's world needed to revolve around me? The people of Tartarus need a leader, I don't deny that, and the lost fae need a leader; it's a fact I cannot challenge because the gods sent these people to her. There is no arguing with the gods.

These people were chosen for Adeena in the same way I was chosen for her, and I've been a fool for not realizing it sooner.

"You're right," I admit. "I am so incredibly selfish for wanting to hold you back from the greatness you have been destined for. You deserve my full support, and from here on out, you've got it. Anything you need, just ask and I'll come running for you."

A sweet smile turns her lips up, and she leans down to plant a kiss on my lips. "Thank you," she says.

Her sweet vanilla and jasmine scent hits my nose as she closes in, pressing her lips to mine. Our lips tangle, twisting and turning together as our kiss deepens. Her mouth opens for me as I slide my hands around her backside, gripping her ass firmly.

A moan slips through her lips as my tongue enters her mouth, and she begins rocking back and forth along my cock. She has nothing under her robe, so her slick pussy rubs directly on my boxers.

"Take them off," she whispers against my mouth.

She climbs off me, then pulls my boxers down my legs as I lift my ass off the bed, allowing her to side them off with ease.

My cock springs free as she uncovers it. Her eyes darken as she licks her lips, eyes focused on nothing but my cock.

She positions herself perpendicular to me as she grabs hold of my cock, bringing it to her watering mouth. Her tongue darts out, flattening as she slides it around the base of my cock. As she brings her tongue toward the tip her mouth closes around it, and I watch her eyes flutter in delight as she moans around it. The warmth of her mouth wraps around my dick, sending shivers up my spine as her head begins to bob up and down.

I grab ahold of the hair close to her scalp, guiding her up and down at a slower pace than what she wants.

Tonight, I want to make love.

I don't need the dirty, filthy sex we enjoy so much. I need to feel the love of my life wrapped in my arms as I tenderly draw the pleasure out of her, sending her into sweet bliss.

Reaching down for her robe, I use one hand to untie the rope keeping it closed. It falls open, exposing her perky breasts. I rub my hand over them as she works my cock, hardening her nipples into peaks. Her back arches and she moans out around my cock as I gently flick her nipple between my fingers.

I pull her head back, releasing my cock from her mouth before she's ready to quit. Staring into her heated, hungry eyes, I growl, "Hop on, and take what you need, baby."

She sucks her bottom lip between her teeth, smiling with her eyes as she nods. Throwing her leg over me, she straddles my hips, hovering over my cock. My cock fills her entire hand as she grabs it, slowly guiding it toward her sopping-wet pussy.

She rubs the head of my cocks along her folds, lingering up high as she swirls it over her clit a few times. Her eyes close as she pleasures herself with my cock, and her head falls back as I lean forward, sucking one of her perfect breasts into my mouth.

I roll my wet tongue around her nipple, lapping at it as it hardens in my mouth. As the peak forms, I flick my tongue over the tip, drawing it out farther. My hands gently massage her ass as she straddles me, spreading her wider for me when she's ready.

She swipes my cock along her folds a few more times, wetting it with her arousal as she slides it deep inside her aching pussy. It clenches around me, tightening as she sits on it, pushing it deep inside.

"Oh gods," she moans, her voice full of desire.

"It's yours, baby. Take it," I groan through intense pleasure as she begins moving up and down on my cock.

Her pussy slides along my pulsing cock with the perfect amount of tight pressure as she quickens her pace. Her breasts move, bouncing against my mouth as she uses me.

I press my index finger into her lips, and she opens for me, allowing me to enter. She sucks my finger just like she sucked my cock, her eyes rolling to the back of her head as she rides my cock. Her tongue flicks around my finger while she moans against it.

She slides her hands between her legs, searching for that tight bundle of nerves. Moving in small circles, she rubs her fingers over her clit as she continues bouncing on my cock. Two of her fingers slide down to meet where my cock enters her, and she tightens them around the base of my cock as it slides in and out.

My hips buck, driving me deeper into her as the pleasure intensifies under her tight grip. She reacts to me, moaning louder as her own pleasure builds inside her.

I'm close to coming, but I need to hold out for her. She's getting closer now. I can feel how tightly her pussy clenches my cock as she nears the edge.

Pulling her fingers away from her pussy, I bring them to my mouth, sucking her perfect juices off them. My eyes roll back as I taste her.

She tastes so fucking good.

She tastes like *mine*.

I suck hard against them, making sure I don't leave a single drop. Her eyes turn molten as she watches me, and she begins moving faster against me, rocking her rips at an angle so that her clit presses against my lower abs.

The pressure builds, and I'm about to come.

She moans with intense pleasure as she tips over the edge, coming all over my cock. Her hips continue moving against me, drawing out her pleasure for as long as she rides the high of her orgasm.

The sound of her satisfaction is enough to send me tumbling into an orgasm, and I begin emptying my seed inside her. She milks my cock dry as her orgasm ends, and we're both left breathless.

Chapter Eighteen

My stomach twists in knots as I stand on the landing overlooking the Fire Court front lawn. Revna and I just said goodbye, and we both cried our eyes out the entire time.

"I have grown to love you as though I would love my own daughter," were her final words as she kissed my forehead, then sulked as she walked back inside the castle.

My bags are packed as full as I can cram things into them, but I'm still missing half my closet. Dreyden watched how frustrated I was getting as I packed, so he promised to bring the rest of my items over in a pocket portal once I get settled in.

Lyra and I will be living in an old manor located on the edge of Northford. At one time the manor belonged to Lyra's grandfather, but just like every other building in Northford, it has been abandoned. She wasn't happen when she found out we'd be going to Northford because it's where all her core memories lie, but she is slowly coming around to the idea of building a new life in a familiar place. Plus, I think she has secretly had her eye on her grandfather's house since childhood, and now it's hers.

I'm nervous.

Nervous beyond belief, but I have to do this. These people need a leader, and the gods have chosen me. The lost fae have followed my direction since the moment they arrived, and there have only been a few hiccups while I established a hierarchy with some of the younger fae. The three boys put on dish duty have been surprisingly low profile since the incident. Regardless of if their behavior has improved or not, I feel a sense of relief knowing I'm taking them out of Fire Court and we can't further anger the Fire Court villagers. Dreyden doesn't need drama started by the lost fae.

I watch the people assembling in the yard. None of them have any real personal belongings. Each of them holds a little bag filled with hygiene products given to them by Fire Court. They've been sent here with absolutely nothing, and Fire Court can't spare more than hygiene kits and a few blankets here and there, which will be carried by the legion.

"Are you ready to go?" Dreyden asks from behind me as he steps out onto the landing. There's sadness in his voice, which breaks my heart.

I'm sad too, but I can't be selfish. I cannot pick my own happiness over twelve thousand lost souls. It wouldn't be right, and the gods would be angered by my decision. They chose me for the job, and I am trying my best to have faith in their judgment.

Reluctantly, I nod. "Yes. Is the legion ready?"

Izan appears in the doorway behind Dreyden. "They're ready when you are," he says as he steps onto the landing.

"It's going to be a long walk," Lyra sighs from beside me.

I roll my eyes at her, nudging her in the ribs. "We've done it before, and we'll do it again. I'm sure it won't be the last."

"That doesn't mean I *want* to do it," she laughs. "But I'll do it for you. I'll go anywhere for the warrior who led me to be a stronger, better woman. It's a bonus you killed Erebus, but I'd do it even if you hadn't."

"If she hadn't, this wouldn't be happening," Izan says coldly.

Tight tension has been strung between Izan and Lyra since we made the decision to leave Fire Court. I think he's pissed off and hurt by her leaving, but he refuses to say it out loud. If I had to bet, I'd say Izan has feelings for Lyra that go beyond what I've seen.

Dreyden laces his hand through mine, kissing it softly as he leads me toward the edge of the stairs. "Your court awaits, *High Lady*."

Icy chills prick my skin as he says the words, and it feels like a sign from the gods. A sign that I'm doing the right thing and this is exactly where I'm supposed to be right now. These are *my* people, and they'll follow me anywhere.

I step forward, holding my breath as I step off the ledge. The life I built in Fire Court was temporary. I'm moving forward, ready to build a life not only for myself but for all these people putting their trust in me.

Our journey to Northford will take several days. We'll set up tents each night to rest, then travel by foot all day long. The legion will be with us for protection, and nothing should go wrong with them there. The Wychwood Forest poses far less of a threat now that the castaway creatures have gone into Sky Court.

My entire plan runs through my head as I follow Dreyden across the field to the front of the legion.

The first decision when it came to leading Sky Court was clear: Lyra would be my second in command. There's no one more deserving or loyal than Lyra, and I can't imagine a better duo than the two badass women who took the Tartarus monarchy by surprise. Since the war, we've tirelessly trained together, and we know each other better than most. She squealed with excitement when I asked her to take on the role, immediately accepting my proposition as she threw herself around me. I'll lead my court with my best friend by my side.

Once we arrive in Northford Alaric will have compiled a list of vacant homes, and we'll get them assigned to each of the lost fae. The land will be divided and a community food plot will be prepared where the previous crops were grown. Lord Weylin from Land Court has agreed to temporarily lend us a few members of his agricultural team. They'll be in Sky Court for a while, teaching the lost fae how to properly prepare the land for farming. He also mentioned they recently created a dense fertilizing solution that we'll be able to spray over our crops to increase the yield by triple.

The lost fae don't have any skills or trades, so everything will have to be self-taught or learned through volunteers from other courts. The few remaining original villagers in Northford will hopefully have a few tricks and trades of their own to help us get set up.

After we've arranged housing, we'll begin to train the new Sky Court legion while simultaneously working to secure the eastern border, the Wychwood Forest. Land, Wind, and Water Courts have already sent teams into Sky Court to begin clearing out the loose creatures. The show of force will hopefully scare looters into hiding, or to at least stop what they've been doing. Our prison will be up and running shortly after we get there, and looters will be placed there appropriately.

More jobs will be created over time. It will be a long, grueling process of trying to fit everyone into an appropriate job that will keep them happy while also making Sky Court self-sufficient again. With time, we'll get there.

A few wildfires were spotted by the specialized teams when they entered Sky Court, and Lady Hali didn't hesitate to send in two more Water Court teams to get the fires put out.

We've worked quickly over the last few days to prepare Sky Court for twelve thousand fae. The Archai courts are working as a unified team to get us in there, and it's all coming together.

It's happening.

Chapter Nineteen

ADEENA

It took us three days to make the journey from the castle in Fire Court to Northford. By nothing short of a miracle, it was uneventful and everyone kept themselves in line. The three boys put on dish duty earlier this week went as far as volunteering to walk at the back, cleaning up as they walked, ensuring sure we didn't leave a trail of trash behind us.

There were no loose or feral creatures to be found. I'm not sure if that's because they're all running amuck in Sky Court, or if it's because they're hiding from the Archai court teams we sent in to round them up. Either way, I was relieved to have a smooth and relatively quick trip.

Dreyden behaved himself the entire way, which took me by surprise. There were several times I caught him trying to take control of what we were doing or what route we were taking, but he promptly self-corrected when he realized what he was doing. Not only that, but he apologized each time.

And he genuinely meant it.

These are my people, and his legion is here to aid us. That puts me in control, which I know is a hard concept for him to grasp, but I think we'll get there eventually.

"So you *are* real," Alaric jokes as Dreyden and I arrive at his family home.

It's such a simple little home, reminding me of the one I grew up in. I don't know if I'll ever be ready to return to Astrari, but I'm sure it's bound to happen someday now that we're back here.

"And so are you," I smile as he takes my hand into his, respectfully bowing to me. "Dreyden spends an awful lot of time here, and I was beginning to wonder if it was a woman drawing him here, but he assured me it's your wife's cinnamon rolls."

Alaric rubs his hand over his stomach in circles, chuckling as he says, "He eats more than his fair share of them when he's here."

Dreyden licks his lips, looking toward the house. "Does she have any?"

Amusement shines in Alaric's eyes. "What do you think?"

Taking off across the yard, Dreyden sprints toward the house, leaving me alone with Alaric.

"He's quite the character," Alaric shakes his head. "You'd think he'd be more mature if he's really four hundred years old."

"Perhaps it's his way of maintaining his youthful appearance," I shrug with a grin. "Do you have the list of vacant homes so we can begin assigning housing to the people?

Reaching into his back pocket, Alaric pulls out a rolled stack of papers. "Of course. I prepared it as soon as I could. I made a copy for your second in command as well."

"Thank you. I'll get them to Lyra so she can begin placing people," I say as he hands me the list. "We were planning on using the old manor house her grandfather owned. She mentioned it overlooked a lake. Do you know if it's salvageable?"

"Hmm," he hums while tapping his chin. "I haven't been out that way for a while, but it was fine the last time I saw it. There's likely damage from the original invasion, but I'm sure it could be fixed up, especially for a high lady," he winks.

"Would you care to take us there after I drop this list off? I would also love for you to show me around the village if you have time."

"It would be my pleasure. I'll be here whenever you're ready to go."

Edlynne immediately took over the task of assigning housing to the lost fae so that Lyra and I could take a tour of Northford then see our new home.

Lyra has been quiet for most of the tour, allowing Alaric to talk about what things used to look like, and how they compare now. Most of the buildings are rundown with broken windows and kicked out doors, but I know a community effort can save them.

I feel sorry for Lyra as we walk. I knew it would be hard for her to adjust to being back here, but I hadn't really put myself in her shoes. Thinking about it is one thing, and seeing her go through it is another. The emotions are clear on her face as her eyes wander the village: anger, sadness, and grief.

It's easy to imagine how beautiful this place once was. The streets are made of cobblestone, and that's a rather luxurious upgrade from Astrari considering the streets were dirt there. Most of the buildings are constructed with a cement and stone mixture, and grand windows once showcased the shops in the heart of the village. It'll take time to restore the village, but now that the looters and creatures are being taken care of, it'll be possible.

A small stream snakes its way through town, flowing with the deepest blue water I've ever seen. It fills a pond near what used to be a park. Visions of children playing in the long grass tickle my mind, and I feel hopeful for the future here.

After our tour Alaric left to help Edlynne. Lyra remembered the way to her grandfather's manor, so she took me and Dreyden there.

The manor sits on the outskirts of the village, positioned by itself overlooking a small lake. The forest sits just on the other side of the sparkling lake. Unclipped grass expands around the lake, and there are several acres of cleared land around the house.

"Oh, wow," Lyra gasps as we approach the house.

"It's gorgeous," I say with wide eyes, taking in the manor in its entirety.

The exterior of the manor is grey stone, complete with a pointed shingle roof and numerous balconies overlooking the lawn. Grand staircases spiral around the front entrance. Half of the windows have been broke out, and that makes me afraid to see what has been done to the inside.

Her eyes are sad as she surveys the house. "My grandmother hosted many balls here. Mostly looking for a suitor for me, but she loved event planning. She never let this place go to waste. It was always shared amongst the community and used as a gathering place."

We climb the staircase to the entrance, and Lyra sighs in relief when she sees the front doors still intact. "My grandfather made these doors himself. My grandmother complained about how cheap the old doors felt compared to the rest of the manor, so he found the most luxurious and heavy would he could, and made her new doors."

Dreyden uses all his strength to force the doors open, slamming into the repeatedly until the latch loosens. "I'd guess these doors haven't been opened since before the war."

Lyra shakes her head. "They haven't been opened for years. My grandparents died long before the war, and we couldn't bring ourselves to come back to the place they loved sharing with us. Most of my childhood memories are here."

Dreyden enters first, cautiously glancing around the house as he steps inside. Lyra follows him closely, suddenly eager to take a look around. I don't close the doors completely once I'm in out of fear we may not be able to get them back open.

There's dust and an overwhelming number of cobwebs covering absolutely everything inside the house. Broken vases spread sharp ceramic pieces across the marbled floors, and we have to watch our feet as we make our way through the house. If the sun wasn't setting right now it would be easier to see the interior of the house, so I'll have to wait until morning to do the extensive exploring I'm planning on doing. Everything about this place is grand and expensive. Archways lead from room to room and pillars support the ceiling where it extends far above my head. We pass at least three sets of spiral staircases, and eventually find what used to be guest sleeping chambers.

Dreyden does a quick sweep of the house as Lyra and I settle into rooms across from other for the night. She didn't say much after we got inside the house, but she explored the house more than I did. She knew her way around well, and I noticed she avoided certain areas of the house on purpose.

I slip into one of Dreyden's oversized tunics before crawling into the bed sheets I just fluffed and dusted.

The door groans as Dreyden opens it. "The house feels clear, but it's so big there could be someone hiding here and I wouldn't know it unless I spent hours going through it room by room. I feel comfortable with us going to bed tonight without a full sweep, but I'd like to do one tomorrow. How does that sound?"

I trust his judgment, and I know if anything were to happen we would be able to take care of ourselves. I haven't been training all these months for nothing.

"Yes," I smile, patting the mattress beside me. "Come to bed."

He slides his tunic over his head then unbuckles his pants, quickly wiggling out of them. He looks stresses as he slides into bed beside me, exhaling loudly.

My brows furrow as I watch him. "What's wrong?"

Crossing his hands over his chest, he turns his face to me. "I don't like knowing you'll be living in such... poor conditions. It scares me seeing the windows broke out and décor smashed to pieces. I've seen it all before, but it's different when I have to think about you living here."

"I think there's a lot of potential here, and it'll provide jobs to get this place cleaned up. It'll take time, I know that, but I know it will be worth it. The yard is large enough to host everyone we brough over and more. Endless bedrooms will be perfect for guests. We can swim in the lake out back." I nudge him gently, "We love swimming."

He's quiet as he listens to me, and I think he's trying to avoid stepping on my toes. His voice has a hint of sadness as he speaks, "We'll get it cleaned up as soon as we can."

Satisfied with his answer, I roll to my side, nestling up against the hard pillow. "Thank you for getting us here," I whisper into the air.

"There's no need to thank me. You know I'd do anything for you."

AN EAR PIERCING scream tears into the bedroom, startling both me and Dreyden from a deep sleep, a sleep far deeper than we should have been sleeping on our first night here, but we were exhausted and passed out quickly.

Dreyden and I react without thought, leaping from our bed as we race toward Lyra's screams.

"LYRA!" I scream as I run, reaching the door just behind Dreyden.

Her cries for help continue, and we cross the hallway, breaking through the door to her room.

My eyes immediately land on Lyra shrieking in the far corner of the room. Her arms are curled tight against her body, and she's holding onto herself as she shakes.

Dreyden sees them before I do, and he's stalking toward the two men lurking in the shadows. Fire lights along his fingertips as he stomps toward them. His fire illuminates the room, glowing against their fearful eyes as he closes in on them.

"We were just looking around!" one of the men shouts.

"You're looters," Dreyden growls as he closes in, grabbing them both by their throats, slamming them against the wall behind them.

The men struggle against his firm grip, clawing at his arms as he raises their bodies off the ground. Their legs dangle, kicking around as they become desperate for air.

I jump over the bed separating me from Lyra, and I grab hold of her. "Are you okay? Did they hurt you?"

Using the flame on Dreyden's hands as light, I search Lyra's body for any obvious signs of injury, but I find none. Gripping her arms, I repeat, "Are you okay?"

There's shock and horror in her eyes and she shakes. Sometimes I forget she's human, and she's far more vulnerable than I am as a fae. Her can-do attitude makes it too easy to forget how fragile she really is.

"Y-yes," she chatters through her teeth. "They were going through the dressers when I heard them. I was sleeping and I didn't hear them come in.

I turn back to Dreyden, and he's still scorching the skin off the two men's necks while he holds them against the wall. He's suffocating them so efficiently they can't even scream. Their voices are silenced as they open their mouths, desperately trying to cry out.

"Don't kill them," I snap at Dreyden.

"Why not?" Dreyden and Lyra bark at the same time.

"They may be looters, but that doesn't mean they deserve death. They clearly did not know we were staying in the house."

Dreyden groans out in frustration, and it's clear he disagrees. "What's your plan then? There's no way I'm letting them go."

"The prison is already being set up. We'll have them escorted to the prison as soon as the sun comes up. Until then, Lyra can try to go back to sleep and we'll stay up watching them. Now please stop burning their necks."

Dreyden jerks his head back toward the two looters, and reluctantly dims his flame. His hands loosen around their necks, letting go of them. They fall to the ground, gasping for air and touching for their necks.

The smell of burnt flesh fills the room, and Lyra begins to gag. I shake my head at Dreyden as I leave Lyra's side, squatting in front of the looters. Holding my hand out, I summon a small amount of my power. The energy buzzes in my hands, and I direct each hand toward a different man. White light slips from my hands, snaking through the air until it reaches the necks of the gasping men. My light wraps around their wounds, seeping into them as I direct them. I heal their burns just enough to take their pain away, but I leave the scars as a reminder of what they've done. Tonight they may have been looting a very recently reclaimed manor, but over the past few months they've likely done far worse.

IZAN ARRIVED EARLY THIS MORNING, and he helped us arrange for the two looters to be escorted to the prison. The travel time from Northford to the prison is a half day walk. Prior to arriving in Sky Court, Lord Soren had sent in a team to get the prison up and running. Volunteer lost fae left yesterday to begin training in the prison.

"I've sent word to let them know the prisoners are on their way. They should get it shortly." Dreyden's tired voice matches his bloodshot eyes.

We thought were exhausted from three days of travel, but staying up all night babysitting prisoners took us to a whole new low.

"You need to teach me how to make my own butterfly spies," I whisper into Dreyden's ear quiet enough for no one else to hear. The butterfly spies are a secret, and I know he'd like to keep it that way.

"I will," he smiles, planting a soft kiss on my cheek.

"We'll get them there promptly, Lady Adeena," one of the escorts says as I hand him the rope attached to the shackles clipped around the prisoners.

"You'll never be accepted here as a high lady," one of the prisoners mumbles as he spits at my face.

A wad of saliva slides across my cheek, catching me by surprise.

Dreyden's fist immediately connects with the side of the prisoner's head, knocking him unconscious. He's already passed out cold as his body hits the ground. The prisoner beside him looks between his unconscious friend and Dreyden, and he shakes his head, trying to hold his hands up in surrender.

Dreyden turns to me with his arms crossed. "You don't have to put yourself through this."

Heat rises to my cheeks. "How can you even say that? This is the life the gods chose for me, and it would be an insult for me to turn my back on that."

His frustration is clear as his breathing gets louder and his jaw clenches tightly. "I'll be out back," he huffs as he stalks off.

I glance down at the prisoner asleep on the ground, then smile at his friend as I say, "Have a safe trip."

The largest of the escorts picks up the limp prisoner, throwing him over his shoulder as he begins to walk. The shackles from the unconscious prisoner yank his friend forward as the massive escort walks away from him. Four escorts and two prisoners leave the yard in the direction of the prison.

For a moment I stand there contemplating whether I should go back inside the manor to check on Lyra and Izan or if I follow Dreyden to the back lawn.

Ultimately, I choose my mate.

Chapter Twenty

DREYDEN

Deep blue water shimmers against the morning sun, and it's easy to get lost deep in thought while I stand at the shore's edge staring into it.

I'm terrified beyond belief.

As each day passes, Adeena becomes more and more serious about staying here. I can't get past this overwhelmingly selfish feeling of wanting her to stay in Fire Court, especially after seeing her here. It's not safe for her and Lyra to be alone here. I can't protect her like I want to if I'm across the continent in my own court all the time.

How will we ever make this work?

She will have her duties to her people here in Sky Court, and I will have my duties to my people in Fire Court.

Is there somewhere I can meet her in between? What's the happy medium here? I rack my brain over and over again, and each time I come up with nothing. I'm paralyzed with fear and I have a hard time processing what's happening. It's all too fast.

Out of the corner of my eye I think I see a small ripple in the water, so I step closer to the water's edge, leaning in for a closer look.

"I thought we were getting over this," Adeena's voice calls out behind me, drawing my attention away from the water.

She reaches my side quickly, quietly staring into my eyes as she waits for an answer.

"I'm trying," I sigh as I throw my hands in the air. "This is the hardest thing I've ever done. Forgive me if I'm having a hard time letting you go."

Her hands land on her hips as her attitude rises to the surface. "There's no need to let go of me when I'm not going anywhere. You can come stay with me as often as you want, and once I get things under control here I'll stay in Fire Court all the time. We'll find a way to make it work. There might be a lot of traveling, but I know we can do it."

"And what about long term?" I snap. "How do you see that working down the road? What about kids someday? You can't tell me we'd force children to travel back and forth like their parents aren't even together. That's unfair."

Before she can respond something comes barreling out of the water, slamming us both to the ground. I'm caught off guard, wincing in pain on the ground as I try to gather myself.

My eyes come back into focus, and I see an onyx hydrol slithering out of the lake, heading straight for Adeena, who's been thrown at least thirty feet away.

In a panic, I begin throwing balls of fire toward the snake-like creature, trying to burn holes in its dark fishy scales. The hydrol shivers as my fire hits it, and it turns its attention toward me as I do nothing more than anger it. Halfway between me and Adeena, it changes direction and comes for me instead.

I continue throwing fire at it, desperately trying to slow it down enough to figure out a plan. Hundreds of years have passed since I've read about hydrols, and I've certainly never experienced one in person.

Adeena gathers herself, planting her feet firmly in the ground as she calls while light to her hands. She throws it over the hydrol's eyes, temporarily blinding it as it closes in on me. I tuck and roll, narrowly avoiding its razor sharp teeth as it lunges for me.

Adeena's while light fades, and the hydrol regains vision only a few feet away from me. It's too late to summon my wings. They'd be crushed of the hydrol knocks me off my feet again, and they'll never unfold in time anyway. I'm looking between Adeena and the hydrol, and I'm coming up blank.

I have no fucking idea what to do.

"You need to move!" Adeena screams, reminding me I'm about to be made into a hydrol's snack.

A shadow from above plummets into the hydrol, and I realize it's Izan. With his sword in his hand, he make a clean slice through the hydrol, separating its head from its body as he lands on top of it.

The hydrol's body goes limp, and black blood begins seeping out of it, coating the lawn in the thick liquid.

"Thanks," I grunt I offer Izan a hand, pulling him off the back of the dead hydrol.

Izan wipes his sword on a spot of clean grass, trying to scrape off the bloody tar. "I saw it in the water from inside the manor. I got outside as fast as I could."

"Two court rulers saved by a second in command? Maybe Izan should be high lord if you can't take care of yourself," Lyra says as she appears on a balcony overlooking the lawn.

"I distinctly remember saving your sorry ass last night," I roll my eyes as I look over at Izan.

And I find him... blushing?

I glance between Izan and Lyra. There's been a weird tension between them lately, and I haven't been able to figure it out, but perhaps this is it? Are there deeper feelings here?

"We're fine," Adeena mumbles as she dusts herself off. "We had it handled."

I open my mouth to argue, but I stop myself.

There's a good possibility she could have handled it on her own, but she wasn't given the opportunity to prove it before Izan shot down from the sky.

I watch Adeena as she flicks muddy blades of grass off her trousers. The way the morning sun illuminates her skin sends chills down my spine.

She's absolutely beautiful, and she's fearless. Admittedly, she's more powerful than I am, and sometimes more stubborn too.

She's Adeena Devna, and she can do anything she sets her mind to. Perhaps she should be here.

Chapter Twenty-One

ADEENA

Dreyden returned to Fire Court two days ago and arrived back this morning. The lost fae ruffled a lot of feathers while they were there, and there are still a lot of unhappy Fire Court villagers waiting for compensation over stolen items and closure knowing justice was served where deserved.

Most of the day he has been busy working on a project with Alaric, setting up the booths at the market in preparation for being self-sufficient hopefully someday soon. They stopped by for a quick lunch at the coffee shop I've been trying to get restored, but they didn't stay long.

Lyra and I have been slowly settling in, and the lost fae seem like they're beginning to settle in too. Everyone seems to be genuinely happy here, and it makes me even more excited for our future.

The manor is coming together piece by piece. It'll be an excruciatingly long process getting the entire place cleaned up. I haven't counted, but I estimate there are at least fifty rooms throughout the manor. That doesn't include the equestrian stable out back, the training arena, the ballroom, or the atrium.

Lyra seems to be relaxing in the house already. Going through it room by room, cleaning up memories of her childhood has been therapeutic for her, and she's finally forced to acknowledge she *can* exist in this place without her grandparents. That's the hardest part for her. Them not being here.

Lady Hali and Lord Weylin have both stayed true to their word, and they've each sent teams in to finish cleaning up wild fires and begin preparation for farming. With the help of specialized teams within each court, the Wychwood Forest border is nearly secured.

The loose creatures are being put back into the Wychwood Forest, and they're killed on site if they refuse to go back.

In my free time, I've been busy cleaning up the streets and buildings in the heart of Northford. Broken windows seem to be our biggest problems, but we've got a trained glazier cutting and installing windows. Several of the lost fae are apprenticing with him, learning the trade, and from what I've seen, they're quick learners.

The lost fae are coming together with the few remaining original members of Northford, creating an incredible community of people. The entire clean-up is a group effort. I get a little emotional watching everyone working together.

Alaric has been a crucial part of our growing community. His son, Razvan, has been a great influence on my dish duty boys, and they've all taken a liking to him.

We called it a day early today, and the boys wanted to play games in the street. They asked some of the older fae to supervise because while the Sky Court is being cleaned up, not all the looters or creatures have been caught. I decided to stick around and watch when I saw them setting up their games.

The boys remind me of the children who once played in the streets of Astrari. Children make a community wholesome, and they keep us honest. These boys plaster smiles across the faces of everyone they encounter, and I can't wait to see their growth over the years here.

Razvan scrapes chalk along the cobblestone, drawing squares in a pattern they'll hop through on one or two legs depending on how many squares there are. It's amusing watching three fae boys play hopscotch with a human boy as confident and sure of himself as Razvan.

"Lady Adeena," a voice shakes behind me, and I recognize it as Edlynne's.

I take my eyes away from the boys playing in the street, turning to meet her frightened eyes, and I'm immediately concerned. "What's wrong?"

She glances around the busy street, her hands shaking as her sides as she whispers, "Can we talk... in private?"

I jump to my feet, grabbing her arm as I lead her inside the small coffee shop I worked on all day. I found unopened bags of coffee grounds, and I've been wanting to use the coffee press.

I point toward a wooden chair as we walk inside. "Sit," I order as I make my way over to the press to make us some coffee while Edlynne has a chance to collect herself.

She's quiet as I warm the water, and I watch her from the corner of my eye the entire time. Her dainty thumbs twiddle in her lap, swirling around as she nervously taps her foot against the white tile.

As soon as the coffee is done I pour it into two white mugs, then offer her one as I take a seat beside her. She looks stressed taking the coffee from my hand, like she's been trying to find words for more than a few minutes. Her hands wrap around the warm mug.

"What's wrong?" I ask again, taking a long sip of hot coffee.

She leans forward with tears in her eyes. "My memory has returned, and others are having theirs return as well."

My lips part as I inhale a shocked breath.

Before I can say anything, she continues, "We were locked in a realm amongst the stars, but there's so much more to it than that."

Chapter Twenty-Two

After receiving an urgent message from Izan this afternoon I had to portal back to Fire Court. Some of the villagers are pissed off that they haven't been compensated for items stolen by the lost fae, but we've been working to take account for what happened and properly distribute funds where appropriate. Several of them refused to talk to Izan, demanding they "speak to the high lord himself."

To be honest, I'm really pissed off I'm even here right now. Adeena had just called a meeting with the entire village, summoning every single lost fae to the manor. She caught me up on her conversation with Edlynne, but I have more questions and I want to be there to support her during her first address to the Sky Court people.

Instead, I'm sitting in my throne room, listening to people bitch and moan about a few gold coins while there are literally people starving to death on the other side of the continent. I'm so sick of dealing with the petty shit when all I want to do it make a difference in the bigger picture.

"You're distracted," Izan laughs as the last person exits the throne room, leaving the two of us alone.

"I wish I was in Sky Court with Adeena. I hate being this far away from her," I sigh as I run my hands through my hair. "I'm fucking stressed."

Izan licks his finger, then thumbs through a thick stack of papers he pulled from his binder earlier. He's so much more organized than I've ever been, and I swear he knows the ins and outs of the court better than I do.

"Let's talk about it then," Izan says as he looks up from his notes.

I shrug my shoulders as I drop my head between my hands, rubbing the back of my neck as I lean forward and close my eyes. "I'm so torn. The people of Tartarus grew on me. The starving children, the regulars at supply drops, Alaric's family... All of them. I even enjoyed hunting down the bad guys if it meant I was keeping the people safe. I felt like I had so much more purpose there. I've spent so much time there, fighting for those people, and coming back here to these whiny villagers makes me nauseas."

I'm on autopilot here. The Fire Court people don't need me, they just want someone to complain to. Izan handles absolutely everything else while I'm away.

Izan tucks his papers back into the binder, then closes it as he looks up at me. "Well," he starts. "Why don't you move to Sky Court? Adeena is your mate, and you need to be with her as badly as she needs to be with you."

I laugh as I shake my head, throwing my hands toward the ceiling and all around me. "Can I just step away from all of this? My home for the last four hundred years? The place I grew up, and the place I know best?"

His tone does not waiver from absolute sincerity when he says, "The choice is yours. I've got it from here if you're done."

And suddenly, everything became clear.

Chapter Twenty-Three

ADEENA

Anxiety pours through me as I ask Edlynne, "What else?"

Her silver eyes almost seem to flicker as she watches me, lightening and darkening as she goes through a wide range of emotions. She swallows, setting her cup of coffee down and then gently placing her hands in her lap.

"We're the Lyke faeries."

I've heard the term before, but I can't remember where. Instead of asking, I let her continue.

"The gods locked us away... In a realm hidden amongst the stars to keep us safe, but we were put there against our will." She leans forward and her eyes blaze bright silver. "I believe our memories are returning because we know *this* place. Sky Court was our home, long ago, when the Tartarus monarchy hunted us. Our powers expand far beyond those of regular fae, and we were a valuable prize for the monarchy at the time."

I'm feeling shock and disbelief. The gods knew we would end up back here the entire time. They released these people not to me, but back to their homeland. "How could the monarchy use your powers?"

Edlynne's face is grim as she twiddles her thumbs in her lap. "They possessed enchanted stones, and they were capable of draining our powers into them. We cease to exist if our powers are completely drained from our bodies. We die. Lyke faeries have more power reserves than the average fae, and we recharge faster. Sunlight feeds our bodies, allowing us to strengthen our reserves with the power of the sun. On a full moon, or close to a full moon, we're able to do the same thing at night with moonlight."

"Lyke faeries feed off the sun and moon?" I breathe.

I've never heard of this, and it barely seems possible, although there are a lot of recent events I would have never thought to be possible.

She nods, her eyes narrowing on me. "In the ancient language, 'Lyke' translates to 'dawn.' We are the dawn fae."

My heart thumps against my chest. It's all coming together now. It's all coming full circle.

Every decision I've made was decided by the gods long before I existed. I'm high lady of Sky Court, and the dawn fae are my people. They fuel their power with the moon and the sun. Everything makes sense now.

Edlynne looks concerned by my lack of words, but she continues as the thoughts spill out of her. "Lyke faeries were locked into the realm as living entities, merely mind and soul, but no body. We've been trapped for over seven hundred years, and every one hundred years the gods allowed us a short glimpse of what life in Tartarus looked like at that time. It was always horrible to see the corrupt monarchy worsen every one hundred years, and we quickly lost hope of ever returning to this land."

"And then they released you shortly after I killed the king..." I say, trailing off deep in thought.

They've been trapped as living entities with no bodies for seven hundred years. They had nowhere to go, and there was no way out. They couldn't even fight their way out because it was physically impossible. The gods kept them hidden from the world for their own protection, but is that not a more cruel form of punishment than death?

What will be the long-term effects of being held against their will for seven hundred years when their memories return? Will they turn on the gods?

"We had no idea what was going on down here. We were somewhere halfway between glimpses of Tartarus, and we weren't aware of your existence or your purpose." Edlynne grabs for the hand I've been using to cup my mouth, shielding her from my utter shock. She draws it toward her, holding it between her two hands. "You are our savior, Adeena Devna. We owe you our lives."

She may feel that way, but what about everyone else? Will they be angry with me for not saving them sooner? If I had known they were locked away, is there something I could have done about it?

My head is spinning as she smiles at me through the silver eyes that closely match my own.

I do my best to collect myself, straightening my back as I sit up. "I think it's time for a Sky Court meeting... with *everyone.*"

Edlynne bows her head as she plants a kiss on the top of my hand. "I agree."

AN OLD CRACKED mirror in the main bed chambers struggles to hold itself together as I watch my reflection. I didn't pack any gowns in my luggage because I chose functionality and comfort over formality, but Lyra sure had. The second I told her of the Sky Court meeting she began rummaging through the assortment of gowns she brought to Northford. Her jade green eyes lit as she found the perfect one, pulling it off the rack and shoving it toward me as the excitement rolled through her.

Word of the meeting is being spread throughout the village, and everyone is on their way to the yard behind the manor. There's a grand balcony overlooking the yard, and I'll use it as a podium to speak to them once they're all here.

"Fit for a queen," Lyra gasps as she returns to the main bed chambers.

I roll my eyes, laughing lightly. "Or a high lady."

The gown she chose is vibrant, perfectly highlighting the colors of the most jaw-dropping dawn. Pinks, oranges, and purples mix amongst white fabric, and there's a shimmery gold dust that lightly coats the tulle strips extending from my waist down to the floor. It hugs my chest and stomach tightly but flows freely from my hips, exposing the stars on my upper thighs through wide slits in the fabric. My ashy blonde hair is twisted away from my face and gathered at the top of my head where it's secured by a gold band. Lyra helped me apply black coal liner to my eyes after she insisted it was necessary to smudge a light pink balm over my lips.

"It's practically the same thing," Lyra smiles with a mischievous sparkle in her eyes.

The gods must been whispering in Lyra's ear, telling her what to pack in her luggage because she is wearing the most gorgeous navy blue gown. Silver and white glitter dust coat the tulle strips in the same way the gold covers my gown. Silver beads bring light to the thick braid running down her back.

She's a midnight queen.

She's my second in command.

Together, we'll rule this court and protect these people from enduring further trauma. They deserve a life of peace and comfort after being cruelly locked away for so long.

"I wish Dreyden was here," I sigh as I approach the doors leading to the balcony.

Shortly after calling the Sky Court meeting, Dreyden received an urgent message from Fire Court and had to return. He was in such a rush he wouldn't tell me what was wrong, but that he'd try to be back by the end of the day.

"We don't need a *man* to ruin this for us," Lyra scoffs as she slips silver hoops through her ears, dramatically rolling her eyes to the back of her head.

Lyra and Izan haven't spoken since we made the decision to leave Fire Court. They both seem to be hurting, but neither of them are willing to talk about it. I tried pushing Lyra to vent, but I only made her mood worse. I figure she'll talk about it when she's ready... she's *very* clearly not ready right now.

A soft knock has us both turning in the direction of the the door. "Lady Adeena?" Edlynne's voice calls out from the other side of the wood.

"You may come in, Edlynne," I say loud enough for her to hear me.

The door knob creaks as she turns it, slowly peeking inside. "Are you dressed?" she asks, shielding her eyes just in case.

I offer her a gentle wave as she pokes her head through the door. "I am. How's it looking out there?"

She steps inside room, eyes wide and glowing as she assesses the two of us. "You both look absolutely exquisite. Your fashion choices perfectly represent not on the court we now reside in, but the people within it. They're going to love it."

Lyra grips the tulle of her dress, swaying it back and forth as she twists and turns. "They are beautiful, aren't they?"

A softness covers her face as she nods, "Yes, they are." She turns her attention to me, grinning as she says, "It looks like everyone is here. From what I've been hearing and seeing, everyone has their memory back. You've got quite the fan club out there, High Lady."

I cross the room to the window, subtly pulling the curtain back to sneak a glimpse of the lawn.

It's overwhelming to see twelve thousand of the most powerful and gifted fae gathered in one place, and it's even more unthinkable to know that I am their leader. They've followed me here, and now they stand together waiting for my formal introduction.

Wandering eyes outside catch me through the window, and one of them men shouts, "There she is! High Lady!" His hands wave and point through the air as he jumps up and down, drawing attention toward me.

"It's the high lady!" a woman shouts from the other side of the lawn, and before I know it there are twelve thousand sets of eyes focused on me.

I step back, catching my breath as I look between Lyra and Edlynne. I don't want to feel nervous, but I am. There are a lot of people out there, and each time I speak to them, they give me their undivided attention. There's a lot of room for error when I address them, and I hope they won't think on it too much if I stutter on my words.

"Adeena! Adeena! Adeena!" the crowd begins to chant, the sound roaring through the side of the manor.

Edlynne giggle as she stands beside Lyra. "I told you there was a fan club waiting for you out there. They've been captivated by you, now go address them."

Doubt clouds my mind momentarily. I shake my hands at my sides, trying hype myself up.

Edlynne sees the hesitation as she watches me. "They'll follow you anywhere, and so will I."

Lyra grabs my hand, then leads me to the wide double door leading to the balcony. "I'll be standing behind you the entire time."

I inhale as deeply as I can, calming my nerves as Lyra and Edlynne each place a hand on the door knobs.

Lyra is all about girl power the last few days, but I'm really wishing Dreyden was here right now. He always knows how to calm my nerves and he's a professional in addressing his people. He makes it look effortless, but maybe that's because he has been doing it for hundreds of years. Perhaps, with time I'll become as graceful with my words as he is, even in front of twelve thousand people.

"Open the doors, please," I request as I straighten my back, forcing my posture into the most confident position I can.

The knobs twist under their hands, squeaking as they turn. A warm breeze floods through the door as it opens, caressing my face as it rushes past us. I exhale as I take a step into the light, revealing myself to the Lyke faeries.

Gasps and wide eyes spread across the lawn as I come into focus, and I can't help but grin knowing this is how they're reacting to me.

The lake glitters in the background, mirroring a blazing sunset. Golds, tangerines, and reds set fire to the sky, battling the incoming darkness.

This is it. I've made it.

I've found my place in the world.

My feet tap against the balcony floor as I cross it, and I come to a stop once I'm directly behind the railing overlooking the law. I rest my hands against it, using it as support to keep my shaking knees from buckling.

As my feet stop moving the people silence themselves, eyes locked onto me like I'm a goddess standing before them.

Applause and cheers tear out across the crowd as I conclude my address to my people. There's hope in their eyes. They're excited for the future we will work together to build, and for the life we have here and now, in this moment.

The widest smile spreads across my face as I wave one last time to the Lyke faeries, turning to hug Lyra.

Except, she's not there, and Edlynne is gone too.

It's Dreyden I find standing just inside the doorway, out of sight of the people on the lawn. He's wearing the most handsome grin, and his eyes sparkle against his all-black formal attire.

"What are you doing here?" I breathe as I walk toward him, still riding the high of speaking before twelve thousand people. "I didn't think you'd be back until tonight. And what are you wearing?"

A black button-up shirt fits tightly against his athletic figure, and black trousers are secured to his hips with an expensive looking leather belt. His shoes are shined to perfection, which is something I've never seen before. He's dressed more formally than the night of the Legion Ball.

There's a glitter in his eyes as he rubs his hands together... nervously?

"I've been doing some thinking," he says, his voice low and inviting as he stares into my eyes. "More than anything in the world, I want to live this life with you. I don't care where, but I know I need to be with you. Most of my time has been spent in Northford lately, and I can't help but think this is the doing of the gods."

"What do you mean?" I ask, my heart pounding out of my chest while I'm unsure what he's getting at.

"I mean... Izan has full control, anyway, right? He knows everything there is to know about ruling Fire Court, and he has been doing a better job at it lately than I have, so why can't he take over?"

He's watching me with the most intense look on his face, and I can't tell whether he's joking.

I'm lost for words, so he continues, grabbing hold of my hand as he falls to one knee. "My purpose is to be here, with you, building a new life for not only the Lyke faeries, but for the people who've been here through it all, the people I've been fighting for six days a week for months on end. You told me it would be selfish for you to stay in Fire Court, and I've come to realize that it would be selfish for me to stay there as well."

I can barely breathe as he reaches into his back pocket, fumbling around before pulling out a small black box. "Dreyden," I whisper. "You can't be serious. You've spent your entire life in Fire Court..."

His thumb rubs against the box, and the top flips up, revealing a twisted metal band topped with a large diamond.

His eyes never leave mine as he gives himself to me. "*You* are my purpose, Adeena Devna. *You* are my reason for breathing every single day, and I can't imagine a life without you. You will lead these people like you are destined to, and I will be by your side, supporting you through it all."

Tears form in my waterline as I wait for him to say the words.

"Will you marry me?"

About the Author

Dana LeeAnn was raised in northern Colorado, where she married her best friend, eventually having two beautiful babies with him. In 2022 Dana moved her family of four to northern Arkansas, where she lives on a fifty-acre farm.

Connect with her on Instagram or TikTok:

@danaleeannhunt.

Did you enjoy *Lady of the Lost Fae?* Be on the lookout for an announcement regarding the third book in *The Starling Series,* which will be the conclusion to this love story! Book four will conclude the series, and it will follow two different characters you've already met.

Acknowledgments

Thank you from the bottom of my heart.

To my **husband**, for being the best friend I could ever ask for, and for listening to me talk about the psychotically dark romance I love to not only read but think up. Your endless support gives me the confidence I need to keep going. This is for you, me, and our future. I love you.

To **Blake and Bailey**, for motivating me to be the best version of myself. I've found my dream, and I cannot wait for you to find yours. I'll be here every step of the way.

To my **grandma**, for being so interested in everything I do, and for loving Blake and Bailey more than I thought possible. I wish I could pick you up and move you here so that I could see you every day.

To **Rocky**, for being incredibly flexible and patient. I promise I'll get my books to you ahead of schedule from here on out!! Thank you!!

To **Giulia**, for designing the most incredible covers, and for making my visions come to life. Your creativity is so special.

To my **betas and author friends** for always providing me with honest and sincere feedback. I am forever grateful!

To my **ARC readers**, for being the best hype team a girl could ask for. Your timely reviews make my life easier, and I can never thank you enough.

To my **readers**, for keeping me on my toes and giving me the best feedback. Sometimes criticism is hard, but I appreciate it more than you know.

Made in the USA
Middletown, DE
05 October 2023